Dear Reader,

Have you ever wondered what it would be like to be somebody different—someone more exciting? I love my life, but there are days when driving my big blue minivan just doesn't seem that glamorous.

Daydreams about spicing up my own life led to Miriam Scott, my chef heroine. Her occupation gave me a great excuse to drool over the pictures in food magazines and look up new recipes! Miriam is about to find out what it's like to reinvent herself, with the help of sexy PR consultant, Dylan Kincaid. I hope you enjoy watching them fall in love as much as I've enjoyed writing for the Flipside romantic-comedy line!

I've been very grateful for the opportunity to share my stories with Flipside readers. And I'm happy to announce that I will soon be writing for Harlequin NEXT, the dynamic new series of women's fiction that launches in July. For more information on my upcoming books, please visit me on the Web at: www.tanyamichaels.com.

Wishing you much love and laughter,

Tanya Michaels

"You think I could be sexy?"

"Absolutely," Dylan said. "We just need some...appropriate wardrobe selections. Like a, er, push-up or lightly padded bra."

"Ah." I experienced a moment of dreamlike panic that, if I looked down, I might actually see my unample breasts *shrinking*. "And maybe I'll be wearing something lowcut to display this new and improved cleavage?"

"This is simply about body lines and what presents the most photogenic form. I wasn't stating a personal opinion, Miriam. Er, criticism. You're..."

Of the two of us, Dylan was definitely the more "unstrung" now. "I'm sorry, I know I said meeting tonight would be a good idea, but maybe I overestimated my—" *Don't say stamina.* It wasn't a word I wanted to think about with him assessing my breasts. "Energy level. I don't think I'm a good subject to work with right now."

He nodded. "Perhaps I'm more knackered than I realized, as well."

Knackered? I assumed from the context that it meant tired. Unfortunately I did know it wasn't the effect I wanted to have on this man....

Tanya Michaels

Spicing It Up

TORONTO • NEW YORK • LONDON
AMSTERDAM • PARIS • SYDNEY • HAMBURG
STOCKHOLM • ATHENS • TOKYO • MILAN • MADRID
PRAGUE • WARSAW • BUDAPEST • AUCKLAND

For Jane Mims,
who shares my appreciation of good food
and has always appreciated my sense of humor

ISBN 0-373-44215-7

SPICING IT UP

This edition published by arrangement with Harlequin Books S.A.

www.eHarlequin.com

Printed in U.S.A.

ABOUT THE AUTHOR

Tanya Michaels has been reading books all her life, and romances have always been her favorite. She is thrilled to be writing for Harlequin—and even more thrilled that the stories she makes up now qualify as "work" and exempt her from doing the dishes after dinner. The 2001 Maggie Award-winner lives in Georgia with her two wonderful children and a loving husband whose displays of support include reminding her to quit writing and eat something. Thankfully, between her husband's thoughtfulness and that stash of chocolate she keeps at her desk, Tanya can continue writing her books in no danger of wasting away.

For more information on Tanya, her upcoming releases and periodic giveaways, please visit her Web site at www.tanyamichaels.com.

Books by Tanya Michaels

HARLEQUIN FLIPSIDE

6—WHO NEEDS DECAF?
28—NOT QUITE AS ADVERTISED

HARLEQUIN DUETS

96—THE MAID OF DISHONOR

HARLEQUIN TEMPTATION

968—HERS FOR THE WEEKEND
986—SHEER DECADENCE
1008—GOING ALL THE WAY

Dear Reader,

For the past twenty months, it's been our pleasure to bring you fun, witty and amusing stories of love gone wrong—and right!—written by some very talented authors. But all good things must come to an end, and we're sorry to announce this will be the last month of Harlequin Flipside.

We want to thank everyone who has written to say how much they enjoy the novels, and hope you'll continue to follow these authors' careers—and find new lines to enjoy—through our Web site at www.eHarlequin.com.

So please pick up a few other titles, grab a latte—or tea, soda or milkshake as you prefer!—and curl up with some wonderful stories about women's eternal quest to find the perfect man. And how she settles on the one who's perfect for her!

Keep on reading and enjoying stories on the funny side of life.

All the best,

Mary-Theresa Hussey
Executive Editor

Wanda Ottewell
Editor

1

It's too easy to fall into a familiar routine that eventually turns stale—whether the routine is in your kitchen, your bedroom or other areas. Sometimes, we gotta spice life up.

—*from the foreword to* Six Course Seduction *by Chef Miriam Scott*

SINCE THAT MOMENT in junior-high home ec when I first realized, "Hey, I kick ass at something," through all the family gatherings where my sanity had been preserved by sautéing in solitude while boisterous relatives drove each other nuts elsewhere in the house, the kitchen has been my refuge. There've been nights on the job when I've actually had the urge to shuffle from the walk-in freezer to the pastry station proclaiming, "Sanctuary! Sanctuary!" But why scare the line cooks?

Tonight, I was using the after-hours serenity for a moment of private victory in the silent, stainless-steel surroundings. We'd wowed one of Charleston's pickier restaurant critics, and the crew had all left for a round of triumphant drinks. I'd taken a rain check, claiming the need to work on a test recipe. From their winks and nudges, it was clear they'd interpreted my excuse as code for clandestine celebration with Trevor. Truthfully, while I don't have one of those "chef's temperaments" you hear about, I had enough ego to want to savor the accomplishment alone.

But I wasn't alone long. "Miriam?"

Startled at the interruption, I glanced up from the pan of ginger consommé I was stirring at the stove. Trevor Baines, whom I'd expected to be working on bookkeeping for another hour, stood shadowed in the doorway. When he stepped into the light of the kitchen, I smiled at how miraculously unrumpled he was in his dark-blue dress shirt and black slacks. The handsome owner of Spicy Seas, Trevor is technically my boss but also my long-term boyfriend. He's tossed around the description "fiancé" once or twice, but we've been too busy with our business plan to discuss wedding plans.

I doubted that was why he'd sought me out now, though.

"We need to talk," he said. Despite our doing a great night's business, his expression was medium dire with a side of pity.

In fact, his features were arranged in what I think of as his Poor Baby face, the one that secretly makes me want to smack him in the head with a spatula. Don't get me wrong, Trevor's a great guy, but from time to time he can be unintentionally patronizing, especially when giving bad news. As if I need to be handled delicately. He should know better than anyone how staid and dependable I am.

My creative culinary bent and occasional errant thought about spatula violence notwithstanding, I was the one who calmly dealt with the behind-the-scenes crises that almost always arise when launching a restaurant. Trevor contributed family money—which secured us the place—and his sweet-talking ability to charm vendors, prospective clients and the staffs of food magazines. His people skills and my fabulous recipes have made Spicy Seas one of Charleston's most successful new dining spots. I have as many insecurities as the next vaguely neurotic twenty-eight-year-old American woman trying to have it all, but my cooking isn't one of them.

I turned off the burner, sensing that whatever he had to say needed my undivided attention. "What's up?"

"First of all, let me just say you did a great job tonight." He ran a hand through his wavy black hair. "You always do, but that critic really liked the wreckfish and spicy fruit salsa."

Wreckfish is a recent South Carolinian delicacy; the salsa, based on tamarind, is a specialty of mine.

"I think the write-up is really going to help us," he continued. Which was all to the good, but his smile had the same ring of insincerity as a doctor who says, "This shouldn't hurt," just before jamming in the hypodermic needle.

"Thanks, Trevor. You know I appreciate the praise, but if there's something wrong, you don't have to soften me up first."

He chuckled. Nervously. "Such a pessimist. What makes you think something's wrong?"

Certain symbols throughout history have been universally recognized as Bad Signs—a skull with crossbones, for example. And the words *we need to talk.* He had to have been really nervous to make such a rookie mistake.

Oh, God. Was Spicy Seas in trouble?

Profits had been promising, particularly for a restaurant less than a year old. Promotion had been well planned, and the critics had been kind thus far. The recent change in seafood suppliers was costing us a bit more, but our new provider's strict attention to conservation principles would benefit restaurateurs up and down the coast.

Don't panic. Whatever the problem was, we would deal with it. My friend Amanda had commented once or twice that she didn't see the sparks between Trevor and me—and we'd subsequently decided that maybe it was better just not to discuss our respective love lives—but sparks or not, Trevor and I made a good team.

"Just tell me what happened," I prompted.

"All right." His hazel eyes were full of anxiety, and he glanced away. "The truth is, I don't think this is going to work."

"The restaurant?" My worst fears, realized. I was certain my face had gone the same white as my discarded toque, the chef's hat I'd removed at closing.

"No, not the restaurant, Miriam. It's doing great. I meant us."

Spicy Seas was doing great—relief bubbled up inside me like milk at a fast boil. Wait a minute, cancel that order. *"Us?* As in, you and me?"

He nodded, suddenly looking haggard in a way that was rare for him even after a double shift. "I think the world of you. You know that."

Well, I'd inferred it, based on our discussing eventual matrimony. Maybe that had been presumptuous.

"You're a talented chef, too," he continued, his Poor Baby expression firmly back in place as he oozed flattery, no doubt meant to temper the blow. "And a, um, lovely person. These months with you—"

"While we're *young,* Trevor." I sounded as impatient and demanding as the most dreaded culinary professor, but allowances for snippiness should be made when a girl's getting…dumped? For a moment, confusion beat out all the other emotions swirling inside. What was going on, and why hadn't I seen it coming? "Is there someone else?"

I had no idea when he would have found time to cheat on me, but I'd watched him charm dozens of women. Women who showed up at the restaurant in little black dresses and the latest haircuts. The combination of hours spent in a hot kitchen and unflattering, boxy chef's whites don't exactly create a *Vogue* cover look.

Trevor shook his head. "It's not anyone else. It's you."

"Me?" I blinked, indignant. Although I could objectively admit he dealt nightly with more attractive women, I still thought he had a lot of nerve to announce that whatever problem we had was my fault. My right hand felt along the countertop for a spatula.

"Not that you've done anything wrong," he hastened to add. "I talk about us during publicity interviews, and it's really made me think about our relationship. You and I together, we don't make sense. Take a rack of lamb—it goes so perfectly with a cabernet sauvignon."

I was too caught off guard by this conversation to point out that the entire concept of Spicy Seas was more imaginative combinations.

"You wouldn't pair it with a cheap beer, right?"

I managed to find my voice. A hoarser, angrier version of it, anyway. "You're calling me a cheap beer. You're breaking up with me *and* insulting me? In my *kitchen?*" He probably had hot plans to crash a convent and harangue nuns next.

Forget whacking him with a spatula, this called for something cast-iron.

"Our kitchen," he corrected with a surly tone no customer would ever hear. "My reputation's on the line with this place. I'm somebody in the restaurant community, among the movers and shakers of Charleston. I want you to stay, of course—you're part of what makes Spicy Seas work—but you aren't the woman people expect to see on my arm."

"Trevor, I…" *Have no idea what to say.* This man who had ardently pursued me now thought I didn't fit his image and should be cast aside like a freaking cuff link that didn't look right with his jacket?

He sighed. "I know there's such a thing as being too blunt, but you deserve the truth. Inside the kitchen, you make some of the spiciest, most creative dishes I've ever tasted. But everywhere else, Miriam, you're a little too bland for me."

WHEN I ARRIVED HOME—a reasonably priced duplex apartment in North Charleston with nice amenities but entirely too little kitchen counter and pantry space—I was still vacillating between shock and anger. Tomorrow, I might be feeling homicidal, or at least angry enough to submit my résumé to Spicy Seas' top competitors. Tonight, though, hours of being on my feet and orchestrating the precision timing of entrées had left me too drained to sustain quality rage.

I pitched my keys on the unfinished wooden TV stand in the living room, then plunked myself down on the striped couch, where I went through the motions of shuffling the day's mail. But I couldn't truly focus on any of the envelopes in my hand, stuck as I was on the unexpected relationship drama that had unfolded. *In this evening's performance, the part of Arrogant Jackass will be played by Trevor Baines.*

I was bland?

Until tonight, I'd been "methodical," which benefited my cooking and was one of the traits Trevor had claimed to like, part of what made us a good match. Trevor had always been more an ambitious dreamer than a doer, although he had been proactive about our relationship. From the beginning, *he* had pursued *me.* Perhaps that in itself should have been a red flag, now that I thought about it. None of the men I'd attracted before—not that their numbers were legion—had possessed Trevor's looks, money and charisma.

Don't get me wrong. I didn't fall out of the ugly tree or anything, I've just never been one to put much energy into attracting attention. Because of my hours sweating in the kitchen, I tended to skip makeup and simply pull back my too-dark-to-be-blond, not-quite-brown hair. My style guidelines came from the health department rather than fashion magazines. Besides, even if I were more fashion-conscious, I'm not exactly a hotbed of potential, with a body just waiting to be draped in the right materials. I exercise frequently to avoid love of food becoming expanse of ass, so I'm not overweight, but I'm not waiflike, either. Or curvy. I have what's politely called "an athletic build."

The no-frills exterior hadn't dissuaded Trevor, though. We'd met when I was working as a sous-chef at an upscale restaurant where the manic executive chef walked out in a prima donna fit one night. I'd received a hasty interim promotion, and Trevor, a regular patron, had noticed the difference. He'd asked to come back to the kitchen and pay his compliments, and we'd started dating soon after.

Now that I thought about it, even his earliest displays of interest had included his conviction that I was destined to be the headliner somewhere instead of an understudy…and hints that he wanted to open a place of his own. Some men schemed to get into a woman's pants. Guess Trevor had just wanted into my recipe box.

I blinked away a fleeting sense of feminine inadequacy, redirecting my irritation to this month's bills. But the dove-gray envelope in my hand said Hargrave NonFiction. My fingers trembled slightly, and I dropped everything else on the mosaic-tiled end table. Although it had originally been Trevor's brainstorm for me to try to have a cookbook published, as a possible promotional tie-in to the restaurant, I'd enthusiastically warmed to the idea. So many months had passed since I'd submitted the pages, however, that I'd almost given up hope of ever hearing back from the publisher. Fine cognacs aged in less time than it took these people to make decisions.

The letter in my hand was thin, and I was half-afraid to open it. Wouldn't good news have come by phone so that we could discuss details? Then again, if it was bad news, what better time to get it than tonight? All I needed were some black balloons and second-rate wine and I could throw myself a genuine pity party.

I scanned over the letterhead and obligatory "Thank you for thinking of us" opener. *They don't want it*. I read the note twice, then wished I'd stopped at the first pass. The upshot was that my recipes sounded fantastic—but people would never discover this if they didn't buy the book, and I didn't have a strong enough marketing hook to stand out among the daunting competition of better known chefs. The editors invited me to try again if I could present a more persuasive selling point, which I took to mean, "Please resubmit if you ever get famous."

It's not personal, I told myself. But it sure as hell felt that way, in light of the double whammy I'd received tonight. My lover found me to be not woman enough for him, and now an editorial committee in New York had deemed me not chef enough. My identity was caving in like a subpar soufflé.

I punched a sofa pillow. Normally, my coping mechanism of choice was a therapeutic cooking binge, but for what it would take to make me feel better tonight, my kitchen didn't have the necessary square footage. I wasn't sure the eastern seaboard had enough square footage. I knew how everyone else in my family handled crisis—talking. They'd talk it out, then do a recap, followed by lengthy discussion of how much it meant to them that they could have these meaningful conversations.

Big with the sharing, my family.

Mom, Dad and my older brother, Eric, have a patent-pending method of baring their souls as quickly and often as possible. If they could get it registered as an Olympic event, the Scotts would take home gold every four years. I picture it as a lot like the luge, but in the three minutes it takes the team to get to the bottom, they'd have to exchange stories on every date, breakup and medical condition they'd ever had. Judges would base scores on technique around the curves and accurate recall of personal details.

Despite my family's manic outgoingness—or maybe because of it—I've always been a little reticent. There used to be tremendous pressure for me to "open up," but then my brother married a woman who filled the gaping hole in my parents' lives, giving them the daughter they'd expected me to be. It's difficult to tell from my twin nieces' frequent inappropriate public announcements whether they've inherited the legacy, or they're just being standard-issue three-year-olds.

I'm thinking they came by it honestly. My sister-in-law is not to be trusted in public. I'd been with her at a grocery store a few months ago, bent down to grab a pack of gum, and by the time I straightened, Carrie had launched into a discussion about breast-feeding with the cashier—much to the chagrin of the elderly man ahead of us in line. I may have temporarily blacked out when the words *cracked nipples* became part of the conversation.

I had to admit, though, that for all my discomfort with the soul-baring Scotts, a sympathetic ear sounded pretty good right now. What I really needed was a sympathetic ear that came with mob ties and an affordable have-your-ex-whacked layaway plan. (I'm kidding, of course. I have my eye on a new set of Calphalon cookware I'd spend money on long before I wasted any funds on Trevor.)

Just this once, I gave into genetic coding and reached for the cordless phone. Lord knows Carrie would be elated if I called her. The dial tone buzzed in my ear along with second thoughts. If I confided in Carrie, everyone who'd ever met me would know about my humiliation by noon tomorrow. Besides, my sister-in-law wasn't part of the Vampire Club—meaning she, like most normal people, would be asleep right now.

Folks who work in the food services and the club/bar scene tend to form a tight-knit group because of our isolating schedules. For instance, my neighbor a few doors down, bartender Amanda White, is my polar opposite in many ways—from her outspokenness to her compulsive dating—but we share the habit of getting home around three in the morning. Over the past four months, we'd become pretty good friends, frequently meeting after hours for breakfast and parting ways before sunrise. Hence the vampire reference, though frankly I'd be lost without garlic.

I knew Amanda hadn't been scheduled to work tonight; would she still be up? Before I even realized I'd stood, I was opening my front door, still clutching the rejection letter. The summer night air was muggy around me, and I clenched my fists as I strode toward Amanda's. By the time I reached her front porch, I'd unconsciously crumpled the paper in my hand to roughly the size of a bouillon cube.

Soft lights spilled through the curtains of Amanda's front windows, so I rapped my knuckles across the door, loudly enough to catch her attention if she was reading in the living room or watching a DVD, but gentle enough that she could ignore it if she was sleeping...or otherwise engaged. She receives amorous offers on a near nightly basis, which, trust me, you'd understand if you saw her. I try never to stand too close to her, for self-esteem reasons.

Footsteps thudded on the other side of the door, followed by a pause. I knew she was glancing through the peephole, and I stood waiting, feeling oddly like a suspect behind a one-way mirror in a police lineup.

The security chain rattled, then Amanda opened the door. Her curly chin-length hair, platinum blond of late, was tousled—very new-millennium Marilyn Monroe—and a pink nightshirt hung to midthigh, her tall, curvy frame making her look like a lingerie model despite the plain cotton. "Hey, Miriam."

"Did I wake you?"

"Course not. I can't remember the last time I was in bed this early," she said, her alert gaze confirming her answer as she backed away from the door.

Once we were both inside, she studied me with a curious expression. "Is everything okay?"

"I, ah… Not really."

She waved her hand to indicate I should follow her into the oblong kitchen/dining room area. Our floor plans were almost identical, but her furnishing was as modern and fashionable as she herself was. She sat in a straight-backed chair at the black lacquered table. I remained standing, restless despite my fatigue.

"You want to talk about it?" she prompted.

Sort of. I mean, that's why I was here, but the words didn't exactly burst forth.

How did my family do this? If I explained how the evening had begun so promisingly, only to end in my being dumped and rejected, wouldn't it start stinging all over again? Wouldn't I sound like a pathetic loser? Clearly, if spilling your guts *was* an Olympic event, I wouldn't make it past the qualifying round.

Besides, although Amanda was arguably my closest friend, we had an unspoken agreement not to discuss Trevor much. He had never hit it off with her, which I'd found ironic considering the huge number of men she did like. It was a little embarrassing to find out she'd been right.

"Mir?"

I stared at her blankly.

"I've got some vino in the fridge," she offered. "Want me to break it out?"

As long as it wasn't the type of cabernet sauvignon you were supposed to pair with lamb. "Trevor and I broke up." The admission got me going—pushed me over the edge and unleashed the building g-forces.

Amanda's memorable violet eyes widened in shock

as I paced around the table, explaining in rapid-fire delivery that I was somehow "too bland" for the man who had proclaimed to love me as recently as... Well, I couldn't *specifically* remember the last time he'd said it, but still! Then I talked about how Hargrave NonFiction, people who'd reportedly paid six figures for the biography of a supermodel's Chihuahua, didn't want me either.

At some point, Amanda poured us each glasses of white wine. Having had practice with people sharing tales of woe over cocktails, she was a seasoned pro at listening. Mostly, she muttered little sounds of encouragement and, where appropriate, a briefly interjected, "That pompous bastard." All much appreciated. When I finally wound down, I slumped into one of the matching chairs, realizing I did feel oddly better. Maybe there was something to be said for this talking stuff out.

But they'd be serving sorbets in hell before I worked cracked nipples into a conversation.

"Wow." Amanda heaved a sigh. "I've never heard you say so much at one time. You're good and truly pissed off."

"You don't think I should be?"

"Are you kidding? I'm *ecstatic*. I mean, not about the rotten night, but everything will work out in the long run. This just gives you the chance to write an even more kick-ass cookbook. And I never was convinced that Trevor was the right guy for you."

After tonight, I was inclined to agree. Who the hell did he think he was? The encounter at the restaurant had knocked me so off balance that his unexpected criticism had temporarily made me feel lacking somehow. Colorless and insignificant. But the only thing wrong with *me* were the hours I'd wasted on an ungrateful egomaniac.

I'll show him colorless.

I slapped my hands down on the table and leaned forward. "You know what? I want to get—"

"Sloshed?" She stood to get us more refills.

My friend, the ever helpful bartender. When life hands you lemons, do tequila shots.

"No. Well, maybe." I was getting there, since I'd been pretty tired even before the first couple of glasses. "But I was going to say *even.*"

"You want vengeance?" she asked as she walked around the counter that separated the dining room from the kitchen.

"Not vengeance." In the past, I'd channeled my emotions into cooking and had come up with some of my best dishes. Now, my anger had taken a subconsciously productive turn. "Vindication."

Bland, huh, Trevor?

Not compelling enough for the Big Apple big shots?

Maybe I could roast two ducks with one glaze.

"I have a plan," I said.

Amanda shook her head. "Can I be like you when I grow up? I'd still be cussing the guy out and cutting up his picture, and here you are already methodically working through your problems and coming up with sensible solutions."

I winced at the word *methodical,* wondering if it was code for boring. "I'm not sure *sensible* is the right word for what I have in mind."

"Ooo…I'm liking the sound of this. Anything I can do to help?"

"Possibly." Even though I'm often more of a loner, I couldn't think of anyone better for helping me brainstorm my bizarre, fledgling idea—the type of idea best mulled over at 3:00 a.m. with a little alcohol buzzing through your system.

"So, what's your plan?" she wanted to know.

I laughed recklessly. "Sex sells, right?"

2

An appetizer is the first impression—that simple yet delicious moment when your eyes meet across the room and *zing!*

Six months later

THE PROBLEM WITH temporary insanity is that it's temporary. Eventually it wears off and you're left with "What have I done?" Such was the case with me this fine afternoon in mid-January.

Spicy Seas was closed on Tuesdays, so I sat in the empty tavern where Amanda worked. Since the bar didn't open until happy hour and the early-shift waitress had called in sick, the place was deserted except for me, Amanda and a hunky bar-back named Todd. They were setting up for this evening's business, and I was swiveling listlessly on one of the stools lined up at the polished teak counter that ran the length of the wall. I glanced past Amanda, a shag-cut strawberry-blonde since Christmas, to the mirrored paneling, trying to reconcile my reflection with the author of the sexy book that would be on shelves at the beginning of February.

What I saw was a woman with stick-straight, shoulder-length hair, a bulky blue cable-knit sweater, and a disbelieving look in her puppy-dog brown eyes.

You'd think I would have adjusted by now to Hargrave NonFiction's remarkably fast decision to buy *Six Course Seduction*—once I'd given them the hook they'd needed, they'd jumped on the idea and rushed it into production to get it out for Valentine's Day marketing. The sale hadn't quite seemed real when I'd fielded the call from my editor saying they wanted to contract the cookbook *and* a follow-up, but I'd started to believe it was going to happen after I'd flown to New York in the fall to discuss the release and promotion schedule. However, any adjustment I'd finally made to impending publication, or to my book's racy new subtitle, had been rendered null and void by the arrival of the dust jacket this morning.

Six Course Seduction: From Hors D'Oeuvres to Orgasm. The cover was currently tucked in the manila folder I'd brought with me, but the image lingered like a visual aftertaste.

While Amanda sliced limes behind the bar, I mulled over *Miriam Scott* printed in immediate large-font proximity to the word *orgasm.* Though I was panicking in reserved silence, my feelings must have been clear in my expression. Or dazed lack thereof.

"You're overreacting," Amanda chided. "I kind of like it."

"Your name won't be on it." I clutched the folder closer to me as if Todd might have X-ray vision.

I had known the publisher would go with a provocative cover, of course. Provocation was the entire point of the chattier revised version, at least as far as marketing was concerned. But not even my editor, Joan, calling to say, "Now, Miriam, don't freak out," had prevented my freaking out.

Against the scarlet background was a neck to midthigh photograph of a curvy and airbrushed nude woman. In place of the slim black censor bars you would see on network television, there were a couple of strategically located food items—luckily nothing as cliché and truck-stop stripper as a whipped-cream bikini. The pictures were starker and more suited to my hot recipes. For instance, the single digitally enlarged habanero serving as a fig leaf. If it had been even a millimeter to the left or right, they would have to sell my book in a plastic wrapper.

I sighed. "You don't look at it and think, porno with peppers?"

At Amanda's snort of laughter, Todd paused in his trek to the back storage room for more ice, sending a brief worshipful glance over his broad shoulder. She ignored the adoring expression, much as she had the other nine million I'd witnessed in the month he'd worked here.

"It's not pornographic," she said when we were alone. "I thought the picture had an artistic simplicity. There are people who would pay good money to hang that in their homes."

"Yeah, but there are people who like instant mashed potatoes, too." No accounting for taste.

She rolled her eyes, handing me a stack of napkins. "Here, make yourself useful."

I began restocking the clustered metal holders Todd would place on the tables throughout the bar's large one-room interior. Maybe Amanda was right about the artwork being tasteful, excuse the pun. The sensuality in the picture could be viewed as understated…in a bright red, naked kind of way.

"What did you think the book was going to look like?" Amanda asked reasonably.

I ran a hand through my hair. "I hadn't got that far yet." Some days, I couldn't even believe what I'd written, much less imagine it in bookstores across the country.

Ever since I'd received the call that my recipes would be published—actively *promoted,* according to the in-house publicist scheduling my upcoming appearances—I'd waffled between pride and the fear that no one in the restaurant community would take me seriously again. Which would be a real problem if the escalating tension at work led to my looking for a new job. Trevor and I had not transitioned well from lovers to platonic employee and employer. We had, however, mastered the intricacies of platonic employee and horse's rear end.

Maybe I should quit, but head-chef jobs don't drop into a woman's lap. And why the hell should I walk away when I'd invested as much as he had in the restaurant? Granted, not in the monetary sense, but in more personal ways. I just hadn't anticipated his recent petty acts of emotional sabotage and passive-aggressiveness.

Now that he no longer had any input on the cookbook, he'd done his best to distance himself from the project. After he'd heard about the racy concept through the industry grapevine, he'd assured me—wearing his best Poor Baby face—that my culinary skills were enough to gain back my reputation if the book flopped and made me a laughingstock. In front of my kitchen crew, he treated me with exaggerated courtesy, giving others the impression that I might still be grief-stricken by his defection and should be handled with kid gloves, which undermined my authority. And he was dating a young blond chef who had worked at a Charleston inn until the place had been mismanaged into a temporary closing, due to reopen in the spring. Clearly Blondie had the image Trevor sought for his love life...and maybe in his restaurant?

"Miriam? Are you aware you're grinding your teeth?" Amanda asked.

I stopped abruptly. "Sorry. Thinking about Trevor has that effect."

Amanda set down her knife, her gaze as sharp as the blade. "Why are you even wasting thoughts on that cad? I know I don't have a lot of experience with sustained relationships, but you can't tell me there was anything there worth missing."

"No, that's definitely not the problem." Miss him? Ha! The more I was around him and his current attitude, the more I wondered how I had allowed myself to go out with him in the first place. It was like looking back on some flavorless, overprocessed, disgustingly fatty junk food you prized as a kid that would turn your stomach if you tried it as an adult.

"So what's up, then?" Amanda prompted. "Come on, talk to me. It's what people do in bars."

I was under the impression people *drank* in bars, but I'd learned my lesson with that months ago, when I'd woken up with a hangover and the outline for a book I was currently second-guessing—half sex advice and half cooking manual. At the moment, I was second-guessing a lot of things. "I'm a little worried that I handed him a golden opportunity by taking off the next few weeks."

My publisher wanted me to plug the book's release with signings in the southeast and a few cooking segments on talk shows. It might not be a full-fledged book tour, but the regional appearances were daunting to someone who had never done any television. Joan assured me a consultant she knew in Atlanta was coming to work with me on media preparation. He'd be here tomorrow. The hope was that, if he did his job right, my public appearances would help sell even more copies, justifying his expenses and paving the way for my as-yet-untitled sequel.

It was all great visibility for me...unless the book tanked and I'd repeatedly linked myself to it up and down the coast.

"What? That toad owes you vacation! You worked nonstop through the holidays." Amanda balled up her fists on her shapely hips, her eyes narrowed and full of the light of battle. Despite any personality differences, she was extremely loyal to me. Might have made life simpler if I could just date *her.* "Not to mention the eighty-hour weeks to help get that restaurant of his up and running. Besides, he can't fire you when he approved the time off. Did he give you crap about it?"

"No, he was eager to approve the time." That's what worried me. "Blondie's gonna be filling in. You think they're edging me out?"

"The place wouldn't last a week without you."

"I suspect he's trying to prove otherwise."

After a moment of silent fuming on my behalf, she shrugged. "You should move on, anyway. Sever all ties with Trevor, date more."

"I've dated." There had even been a couple of kisses good-night over the last six months, but that paltry statistic was more likely to incite Amanda than appease her.

"Barely! I could probably count your dates on one hand, and one of them was nothing more than meeting for coffee. I think working for your ex is hindering your love life."

Funny. I thought being me was hindering my love life. My hours were weird, I'd been busy writing the second book—or at least telling myself I should be writing it—and most of my social circle was comprised of couples Trevor and I had spent time with. Besides, I wasn't the kind of woman who had new guys beating down my door. Even though men *say* they'd love to find a woman who isn't into constant talking and emoting, many of them are unsettled when they do find someone more reserved.

"Well, we can't all be romance goddesses," I answered lightly.

"Better not tell that to your reading public."

Yeesh. She was right—a certain persona was expected. Even the picture for the dust jacket had been an ordeal. The publisher definitely hadn't wanted a headshot of me in a white toque. No, I'd been wearing makeup that made my skin feel heavy, and my mousy hair had been teased into big poofy curls I personally hadn't found any more flattering than my normal do. At least I'd successfully vetoed the photographer's suggestion that I be nibbling suggestively on a piece of chocolate-dipped fruit.

What would the image consultant be like? Just someone who walked me through the basics of a television appearance, or another person who encouraged large hair and fondued strawberries? If so, I hated him already.

"Maybe I'm not the right person for this," I mused aloud.

"For what?" Amanda asked as she double-checked her well, the group of commonly used liquors kept in front with plastic pour spouts attached. In the low-cut, long-sleeved red top she wore tucked into jeans, she would make a killing in tips tonight. I should have sent *her* to New York in my place. And on the publicity tour.

"This book."

"Little late for that now," she said. "Besides, you're the perfect person for the book. You just don't know it yet."

Doubtful. I could talk to people about what went on in their kitchens, sure. No problem. I'm your gal. But I'd bluffed my way through the "bedroom" portion of the manuscript—the part that had convinced my publisher to shell out actual cash.

Discuss sex with strangers? I hadn't been able to talk to my own mother about getting my first period. Rather than tell her, I'd taken quarters to school and stocked up on supplies from the vending machine in the girls' restroom. It wasn't that Mom was unapproachable; quite the contrary, I'd had nightmares about her cheerfully telling the cashier it was my inaugural tampon purchase. It sounds like an exaggeration, but I vividly remember her maternal pride on our one and only mother/daughter bra outing. Unfortunately, twelve department-store shoppers probably do, too.

And it had taken almost a month of friendship with Amanda before she'd finally got the "too much information" message when it came to sharing the details of her romantic escapades. I was not a hotbed of racy gossip.

"Want me to pour you a drink?" She glanced at the wide red-leather watch on her wrist. "We open in five minutes, so it's not really breaking the rules."

"Oh, no. I have to be careful imbibing around you. A few drinks and an encouraging nod later, I could wind up hosting some bad reality show called *Chefs Gone Wild*," I teased. "I blame you for this book in the first place. Friends shouldn't let friends outline under the influence."

"*You* came up with everything," she countered with

an approving grin. "I don't even know any recipes, so it's not like I contributed anything but support."

"Yes, but you've gradually corrupted me—all that bar talk. Sex on the Beach. Sloe Screw. Buttery Nipples." Which, after my initial shock wore off, I discovered was a butterscotch-flavored shot. "And Screaming-Up-Against-the-Wallbangers."

She laughed. "That belongs in the *Bartender's Guide to Mixed Metaphors.* Come on, now. You are happy they're releasing your book, aren't you?"

"Giddy."

Actually, for all my misgivings, I'd worked hard on the cookbook. If I hadn't proved whatever point I'd set out to make, I'd still given a lot of thought to my culinary instructions and was thrilled to get it in front of people. It's just that while I'd been penning chapter three, "Soup, Salad or Me?", I hadn't considered the reality of anyone actually picking up a copy and *reading* it. My remarks to the public on how to spice up their cooking and their love lives would be displayed in stores across the country.

I groaned. "Little old ladies are going to see it!"

"Hey, little old ladies deserve to get some, too."

"The sex part was a marketing ploy," I reminded my friend. "The book's about great food."

Amanda's violet eyes sparkled. "I meant great food."

"Sure you did."

A knock sounded against the locked glass door at the front of the room, and Amanda came around the bar to answer it. But Todd emerged from the storeroom before she'd gone very far.

"I'd be happy to get that for you," he said soulfully. With that tone, he could have as easily said, "I'd be happy to take a bullet for you," or "I'd be happy to father your many children."

As he disappeared toward his left, to the entrance that wasn't visible from where we sat, I turned to Amanda. I hadn't said anything about Todd since I'd met him, but couldn't help myself now. This was getting ridiculous.

"You know he's crazy about you?"

"It's just one of those older-woman crushes," she said dismissively.

"He's what, two, three years younger?"

"Still." She leaned against the bar stool next to mine. "He's not…I mean, he's awfully boyish. I'd feel all, 'Mrs. Robinson, you're trying to seduce me.'"

I laughed. "With that outdated reference, you *are* old."

But I knew what she meant. I wasn't sure why I'd even broached the subject. Maybe her needling me about my slow love life had made me realize how uncharacteristically long it'd been since she'd mentioned hers.

"You aren't seeing anyone these days, are you?"

She started, her eyes wider than normal. "Why do you ask?"

"Seems like it's been a while since you were telling me about the guy you're involved with or want to be involved with or are dumping after your brief but torrid involvement."

"And you're complaining? I thought you didn't want to talk about stuff like that."

Her casual tone seemed forced, and I wondered in a surprising flash if I'd hurt her feelings during some previous conversation. "I don't need to hear every guy's exact talents and proportions, but I'm still interested in who's who in the life of Amanda White."

"Oh. Good to know." Her smile was rueful. "I'll keep that in mind for the next time there *is* a man."

Speaking of men.

Wow.

Todd had reappeared, jangling the keys to the main entrance door, and behind him—did I already say wow? The patron who'd come inside from the cold was tall with golden-blond hair, striking features, piercing eyes that I was pretty sure were green, a black leather jacket and dark jeans. Literally everything about him made me want to volunteer to warm him up. And I do not mean with my signature cayenne-spiked gourmet hot chocolate.

I can't even explain what made him so…let's just say he had a quality. Certainly he had a gorgeous face, complete with a strong chin and jaw that proclaimed masculinity and strength and decisive power. From what I could tell, he also had an amazing body beneath the charcoal knit sweater and perfectly sized jeans, neither tight nor baggy. But it wasn't any of those things that turned my knees to custard. It was the overall impression he created, something about the way he carried himself. Trying to define it would be like trying to properly explain the taste of truffles to someone who's never had them.

Standing next to me, Amanda let out an appreciative sigh, and I figured my days of not hearing about her love life were over. Jealousy scalded me, but I smiled in her direction as the source of our mutual—*cross-eyed, drooly lust*—admiration came toward us.

"He…" She shifted her weight from foot to foot, and I doubted her breathy tone was due simply to keeping her voice low.

"Has a certain quality, doesn't he? Sensual. Confident. Powerful."

"Jumpable." She cut her gaze to me. "And, damn, do you need a man."

This was why I was a chef and Amanda microwaved most of her meals; she wasn't big on savoring.

"Ladies." His deep voice was rich, as velvety as a perfectly prepared roux. His smile held none of the arrogance I'd sometimes glimpsed in Trevor when he realized women were checking him out.

"Hello, there." Amanda had the presence of mind to flash an answering smile. My greeting so far consisted of openmouthed ogling. "Can I get you something to drink?"

"No, thank you." He frowned at her. "Do you work here? I thought... Are you Miriam Scott?"

Amanda's gaze whipped toward me, and I could feel her shock. Or maybe what I felt was my own shock. This man had sought *me* out? On purpose?

My heart accelerated when I spoke to him, in that nervously infatuated way I'd assumed people outgrew after puberty. It was difficult to get my pulse back to normal when I was reeling from the surprise of a gorgeous stranger appearing and asking for me by name. "That's I'm. Me. I'm her. Miriam."

Was it too late to take Amanda up on her offer of a drink? A gin and hemlock would hit the spot.

The stranger's green eyes widened. "*You're* Miriam? Oh. So sorry about the misunderstanding." For a millisecond, his puzzled frown not only lingered, it deepened. But then he replaced it with a polished smile. His arm snapped up at the elbow, suddenly bent and extended toward me so that we could shake hands. "Dylan Kincaid, here to get you ready for public appearances."

He was professional enough not to say what I'm sure all three of us were thinking: *And, Lord, do we have work to do.*

3

Homey comfort foods definitely have their place, but are they enough to satisfy you? Rich, exotic pleasures are more accessible than you think.

LIKE A PANICKED GENERAL trying to rally the troops, I gathered my thoughts. I needed everyone to report for duty *now.* "Mr. Kincaid, it's a pleasure to meet you."

I braced myself for the handshake, vowing not to dissolve at his touch. His palm was warm, but not soft, and his fingers wrapped purposefully around my hand. *Can I be your love slave?* Amanda was right, I did need a man.

"I wasn't expecting you until tomorrow," I managed to choke out, awarding myself points for remembering to let go of him.

He smiled apologetically. "I hope I'm not inconveniencing you by arriving early. My previous job ended sooner than expected, and Joan mentioned you were a bit nervous about the promotional events."

His eyes warmed affectionately when he mentioned my editor, and suddenly I wondered what she'd meant when she'd said she "knew him."

"I stopped by your house," he continued, "thinking that if you weren't home I could check in to the hotel and then try your restaurant, but a neighbor told me you'd be here."

I nodded. That would be Mrs. Asher, widowed busybody who would no doubt quiz me about the handsome stranger later. "Spicy Seas is closed on Tuesdays, so I was keeping my friend company." That sounded better than admitting I'd shown up here needing reassurance that my book wasn't porn. "This is Amanda White."

"Very nice to meet you," she said in a voice that stopped just shy of a purr. At my sidelong glance, she cleared her throat. "But I guess I should be getting back to work."

I'd been so intent on Dylan, I honestly couldn't have said whether or not the first customer or two had trickled in now that the door was open. I waggled my fingers in a half wave at Amanda as she left us alone. Something about Dylan...

"I'm sorry, but have we met?" I asked.

My question may have sounded like an excuse for further staring on the pretext of trying to place him, but there really *was* something hauntingly familiar about him. The further staring was just a bonus.

He shook his head, the godlike aura of confidence dimming for a moment, as if my question had made him uneasy. "No, I haven't had the pleasure."

Even though I was sure he was right, the undeniable sense of déjà vu remained. Oh, well. Maybe any sane woman would have experienced this I-know-you-from-my-dreams spark.

"Why don't we sit at one of the tables?" I invited. "We can talk about the tour schedule and what I need to do to prepare."

"A sound plan."

I told him I was just going to grab myself a soft drink before joining him. Declining a drink of his own, he stepped up into the railed-off side section that ran alongside a small dance floor. Watching Dylan drop his leather jacket over the back of a curved café-style wooden chair, instead of looking where I was going, I nearly collided with Todd as he circled the room to distribute the napkin holders and stacks of cardboard coasters.

When I reached the bar, I discovered I wasn't the only one who had trouble tearing her gaze from the newcomer.

"I can't believe your luck!" Amanda said. "Putting yourself in his hands for a few weeks? Mmm. When you said your image consultant was a man, I was expecting..."

"What?" I hadn't given him much thought, too worried about what he'd think of me. Although, the word *consultant* had conjured vague images of a suit—maybe someone with wire-rim glasses who didn't smile much. Instead, I got a honey of a man with deep green eyes that crinkled at the corners in tiny, sexy laugh lines when he smiled.

Amanda shrugged. "Well, how many men are renowned for doing makeovers on women? I think I pictured someone a little more Queer Eye for the Publicity Shy."

"Amanda! What a stereotype." Although, except for relying on further stereotypes, we had no way of knowing what his preference was. I pushed the thought aside, currently unable to bear the notion of Dylan Kincaid off-limits to women. "Guys can be fashion conscious and trendy. Trevor, for instance..."

Then again, I sincerely hoped Dylan Kincaid was nothing like the ex who had punted me from his heart and, given time and opportunity, possibly his restaurant. "Never mind. Just give me a diet soda before he wonders what I'm doing over here."

I carried my drink to the table, at half my usual pace because all I needed to truly impress the guy was to trip and spill soda all over myself. Was Amanda right about this being a makeover? I hoped Dylan's advisory capacity would be more akin to a Toastmaster's tutoring, getting me ready for public speaking. The prospect of his prescribing heavy cosmetics and high heels made my stomach drop.

My expression must have conveyed my uneasiness, because he smiled as I sat across from him. "Don't worry."

"Is this where you assure me you don't bite?" I asked, lifting my glass to my mouth.

"Actually, I do," he drawled in a wicked tone. "It just doesn't hurt."

I choked on the soft drink, coughing as the unique sensation of carbonated bubbles stung the inside of my nose.

"My apologies," Dylan said, his gaze sheepish. "I didn't mean to alarm you, it was just a demonstration."

"Of the inherent dangers in carbonated beverages?"

He laughed. "Of the kind of attitude you'll want. I haven't read your book yet—Joan's expressing a copy to me—but I've discussed with her the content and tone. What you'll need to project is a flippant, sassy magnetism."

Uh-huh. No wonder he'd thought Amanda was the author.

"Um, Dylan…maybe you've noticed how I don't exactly radiate a come-hither persona?"

"That's what Hargrave is paying me for."

It was going to be big hair and oral sex with strawberries all over again, I just knew it. "You know more about PR than I do, but isn't promotion more successful when the subject is herself?"

That's what you always hear: be yourself. Unless "yourself" was me.

"But you will be," he said. "You wrote the book, right? So it's in there. I'll simply help you bring it to the surface a bit."

A bit? I had the feeling it would be more like raising the *Titanic*.

I CANNOT DO THIS. Even as I thought it, I called myself a coward. This was my family. Not a den of serial killers.

But standing on my parents' creaky wraparound porch Wednesday night, I found myself physically unable to press the doorbell. Partly because balancing the cardboard box of hardcover books was no easy task, but mostly because handing over the first copy would feel a lot like walking naked into a crowded room. I tried to focus on the positive, reminding myself that my family's seeing the book in private surroundings might tone down some of the fuss they were bound to make in stores.

Originally, I'd scheduled my leave of absence to begin today because I assumed I'd be working with Dylan. But he'd called this morning to say Joan had sent him a copy of *Six Course Seduction*. He wanted to read it before we met again so he knew exactly what we were trying to sell with these publicity visits. At loose ends, I'd accepted Mom's invitation to dinner, relieved that I had more time before I had to face the hot consultant again. January or not, thinking about him made me want to turn on the air conditioner.

I'd been fairly surprised to receive my own box of

books from Hargrave this afternoon—why bother sending me a copy of the cover when I'd get to see the real thing twenty-four hours later? But it was no stranger than them overnighting me a set of giveaway pens for a book signing still weeks away, while they sent more important mail, like my contract, by Pony Express, using what I could only assume was a lame pony with no sense of direction. Publishing logic was a mystery to me.

The door of the two-story house swung open suddenly. Carrie stood on the other side, a confused expression on her round, pretty face and a twin balanced on one ample, khaki-clad hip. My sister-in-law is beautiful, but in a different way than Amanda. Carrie has this quintessential-woman glow about her that inspires men to take her home and try to make babies.

"What are you doing standing out here, sweetie? If you needed help with the box, you should have come in and asked Eric to get it." She glanced over her shoulder past my parents' living room. "Eric! For pity's sake, get out here and help your sister."

I started to tell her assistance wasn't necessary when my brother, a middle-school teacher, appeared in the hallway behind her. He claims he's put on a few pounds in the last couple of years, but they're well disguised on his six-two form. We don't look much alike, my brother and I. Aside from the height difference caused by my very average five foot four, Eric has Mom's blue eyes, and his hair is a few shades darker than mine, so that it's legitimately brown. Plus, I don't have glasses. Or a goatee.

Eric held a small pink towel and dried his hands as he walked. "I was in the bathroom. Give a man a break."

Carrie rolled her eyes, scooting out of the doorway. "You're always in the bathroom. And that better not be one of your mother's guest towels."

Eric shot a guilty look at the scallop-edged terry cloth. "Technically, we're guests."

I lugged the books as far as the entryway floor, then shut the door behind me. My niece, a dimpled tow-headed cherub who looked like mini-Carrie in overalls, scrabbled down from her mother's grasp and barreled toward me on unsteady legs. Coordination probably improves with age, but right now, my nieces are propelled by more enthusiasm than grace.

She tackled my legs in what was either a hug or a desperate attempt not to hit the floor. "Aunt Mi'am!"

I scooped her up, ninety-nine-point-nine percent sure this was Lyssa. Her identical sister, Lana, is just a fraction more reticent and, as such, my secret favorite though I would never vocalize a preference, even upon threat of pain. Or, worse, greasy fast food.

The four of us went toward the back of the house, past the staircase that led up to the bedrooms, following the murmur of the evening news and the sound of Lana giggling at my father's tickle-monster growls. The large kitchen, which had given me some of my best memories in this house, took up the entire right half of the floor plan. To the left was the living room in which we're actually allowed to sit. The fancy sofa in the front room still has plastic on it and, guests aside, Mom hasn't allowed one of *us* to take a beverage in that room since the grape juice spill of 1986. My gregarious parents are free-spirited in many respects, but my mother was born and raised in the South and takes her visiting parlor seriously.

The crisp cinnamon aroma of warm apple pie

greeted me at the same time as my mom, her face flushed. She tells everyone, strangers included, that she spends as much time cooking as possible so people will think she's overheated from baking instead of menopausal hot flashes. "There she is! Our daughter, the soon-to-be-famous author."

Or soon-to-be-infamous. "Hey, Mom. Thanks for asking me to dinner. I can't believe you forbid me to bring anything." Though she obviously needed no help on the dessert front, I would have been happy to bake some bread or whip up a special vinaigrette for the salad.

"When you invite Michelangelo over, you don't ask him to paint your garage," my father proclaimed, walking into the room with Lana on his shoulders. He was a hearty bear of a man, undiminished by age, and in his crimson university sweatshirt, he looked almost young. Except for the dashes of silver in his close-cut sandy blond hair.

My mother waved me toward a well-worn kitchen chair. "Sit, sit. Tell us more about this tour. You mentioned your consultant has come to town?"

"Oooh." Carrie took the seat next to me. "Will you get your own hair and makeup people, too?"

"I don't think it works exactly like that." Hargrave had already invested in Dylan's fee, which I knew was far more financial backing than many authors got. I was investing some of my own money in promotion and image, too, of course, but I was hoarding as much of the advance as possible, the specter of unemployment looming in the back of my mind. "He's just here to help me polish my image before I go on television."

My father lowered his granddaughter to play with her sister. With Lana in pigtails and yellow overalls and

Lyssa in a ponytail and pink jumper, the girls looked like bookends.

He straightened, beaming at me. "Your mother and I plan to videotape every single appearance."

Nothing said pressure like knowing any gaffe you made would be forever accessible through the modern miracle of rewind. "That's…sweet of you guys. But not all of it will be local."

Some of the cable shows—mostly of the Good Morning variety—were in neighboring states like North Carolina and Georgia and would only air within a certain radius. I was trying to wrap my mind around the task of being coherent at seven in the morning, much less sassy and sensual. Shudder.

Dad headed toward the stove, inhaling the fragrance of Mom's slow-cook spaghetti sauce. When he picked up a spoon and nudged aside the blue pot lid, however, Mom brandished a plastic spatula at him. (So *that's* where I get it from.)

"Stay out of there," she ordered. "You'll end up double-dipping and sharing your germs with everyone else."

Nice to know my family drew the line at sharing something.

As we all pitched in to set the table, I answered questions about the book, even though most had already been asked on previous occasions. Yes, it would be available at all the major bookstores. No, I didn't expect to become a household name. Yes, I was a little nervous about the interviews, and yes, I still planned to keep my job at Spicy Seas. Granted, that plan was growing more tenuous by the day, but I kept the thought to myself—a concept rarely witnessed under the Scott roof.

"You're sure it's such a good idea for you to work

there?" my mom asked as she piled noodles on a daisy-print plate. "That Trevor broke your heart."

"Not really," I mumbled from the refrigerator, where I was pulling out store-bought salad dressings.

"No need to put on a brave face for us," Carrie said. "If you ask me, he behaved like a complete j-e-r-k."

I chuckled at her rated-E-for-everyone editing. If she was going to go to the trouble of spelling out the word, she might as well have used one of the doozies.

"But the two of you were together such a long time," my mother pressed. "You were planning a wedding!"

"*Planning* to plan a wedding, Mom." Sure, we'd been busy with the restaurant, but I saw now that he'd been in no hurry to take our relationship to the next level. Neither had I, to be honest.

"We're here when you finally decide to talk about it," my father chimed in as he buckled Lana into one of the two high chairs. My dad was an exception from a generation of men known for limiting conversation to grunted monosyllables during the commercials of televised sporting events.

"Thanks, Dad. But it's been six months. I think I'm pretty well over it."

"Wonderful," my mother said, as we all sat down. "Then you'll have a new man in your life soon? We're anxious to hear all about him."

Thank God my mom is the person from whom I'd inherited my cooking skills—no one could resist digging into a meal she'd fixed, which gave me respite from all the well-meaning conversational prompts.

With equal parts ceremony and exaggerated patience, everyone waited until after dinner before they began demanding a peek at The Book. "We fed you first because we didn't want to be rude," Mom said, as we cleared the table, "but the suspense is killing us!"

Nods of assent came from all around the kitchen, general agreement that I was risking their collective lives.

"All right." I shoved my hands into the back pockets of my jeans. "But don't feel like you *have* to read it. I mean, if cookbooks aren't usually your thing, anyway, I don't want you to think that, just because I wrote it, you're obligated—"

"Nonsense," Dad interrupted. "My little girl is having a book published. I for one will be reading it cover to cover."

Shoot me now.

"And I'm ordering dozens of copies," my mom added. "I'll give them out to everyone I know!"

That should make for quite the Ladies' Auxiliary meeting.

I went to the foyer and picked up the box, which seemed even heavier than I remembered. I'd no sooner set it on the kitchen table than four pairs of hands reached for the flaps and began extracting copies. My brother got the first one, and his eyes widened at the bright red cover. Lyssa stood on tiptoe to peer curiously over the edge of the table, and Carrie reached out one hand to shield the three-year-old's eyes.

"Is she wearing anything?" My father, sounding more intrigued than judgmental, stared at the book Eric held.

"Food," my mom answered, pulling out her own copy.

"Well." Eric grinned. "Nice rack…of lamb." He's often said that being stuck in permanent adolescence is what helps him relate so well to his students.

"Hey!" Mom had opened her book and was inspecting the dust jacket. "There's a picture of Miriam in here."

"Is *she* wearing anything?" Eric smirked in my direction.

My father smacked him in the shoulder with one of the author copies.

Carrie had taken the nonlinear approach of randomly flipping through pages and was reading aloud. "Brownies to Bring Him to his Knees, or any other position you want him in."

Eric wolf-whistled. "Mom, Dad, maybe you could keep the girls for a weekend sometime soon?"

My cheeks heated. Somewhere in America, there must be parents who would be mortified by their daughter writing *Joy of Cooking* meets *Joy of Sex*, but not in this kitchen.

"I wish you'd written this a couple of years ago, honey," my mother said. "Your father went through this period where—"

"Mother!" I jolted out of my chair, thinking *oh, the humanity*. "I will never ask you for another thing if you promise not to finish that sentence."

She blinked at me. "Sorry. I was being supportive. I'm really excited about this book, and the tour. It's all so unlike you!"

As complimentary as she'd no doubt intended that to be, it somehow felt like a reverse insult.

"Absolutely," Carrie chimed in. "You've always been so closed off, sweetie."

Closed off? Because I didn't discuss my sex life over dinner, or sit around asking everyone to analyze a weird dream I'd had or, as Eric was wont to do, pick up a newspaper and make an announcement whenever I headed for the restroom?

When my cell phone chirped, I dove for my purse like a carb-addict for the last croissant. "Miriam Scott."

"Miriam, it's Dylan." His voice poured across the line, whiskey-smooth. "Is this a bad time?"

"In the course of history, there has never been a time this good."

There was a pause before he chuckled. "Right, then. I wanted to let you know I finished reading your book."

"Oh." And what had been *his* reaction to "Brownies to Bring Him to his Knees"? I wasn't sure I wanted to know.

"I don't want to interrupt your evening, but you said you were accustomed to keeping late hours. I'm a night owl, too, actually, so if you aren't otherwise engaged after the family dinner, would you like to get started tonight? We could meet at your place. You'll probably be more comfortable there than at my hotel, and we'll need somewhere private for the videotaping."

He'd explained last night that one of the first things we would do was tape me, then work from there once we'd viewed the results. *Won't that be fun?* I hadn't been this excited since my root canal in college.

"Or," Dylan said when it became clear that my unenthusiastic silence was stretching on with no end in sight, "we can start fresh in the morning. Entirely your choice."

Spend time with the man who left me tongue-tied, sweaty-palmed and aching to follow every piece of advice between the pages of my book, or stay here and be further traumatized by mental images of my parents' love life. "How soon can you get to my place?"

4

The way to a man's heart is through succulent breasts: Five mouthwatering chicken recipes.

ONCE DYLAN AND I had agreed on the estimated time we both thought it would take us to meet at my apartment, I hung up the phone, struggling to look apologetic about my excuse to leave. My family was understanding, but Mom delayed my departure by insisting she should pack food for Dylan.

"I'm a chef," I reminded her. "You don't think I'm capable of feeding a guest? Although it's probably a moot point, since I'm sure he's eaten dinner by now."

"So he can have dessert," she said as she flipped open cabinets, searching for a travel dish for what was left of the pie. "Don't underestimate the power of winning a man through food."

"How could she?" Eric asked from the table. "She wrote the book on it!"

I groaned in my brother's direction. "Why again would having a man in my life be a *good* thing?"

Carrie shoved plates in the dishwasher, laughing. "They have their uses. Let me know if you change your mind about wanting one... We have some friends coming in tomorrow for a wedding this weekend, and I think Michelle's brother is single. Want me to pass on a copy of the book for him? It would give him a glimpse of your picture and your personality, and I can make sure Michelle knows you're available."

"That's not necessary." Just what I wanted a guy's first impression of me to be, the big-haired photo and an entire section titled "Asparagus: A Phallic Side Dish with Stamina." All that *plus* hints that I was looking to hook up with a stranger? Pure class.

It took a little longer than I'd anticipated to say goodbye, kiss both of my nieces and carry the book box, minus a half-dozen copies, and a plastic container of pie out to my car. I drove home using a somewhat loose interpretation of the speed limit, suddenly aware that my comfy sweatshirt and scuffed jeans weren't necessarily the clothes I wanted to be wearing to greet Dylan.

Since he was here to consult with me on creating a sexy image, it would be nice if I at least gave him some potential to work with.

Once inside my apartment, I barreled toward my bedroom. I slid open the mirrored door of my closet, eyeing the contents with indecision. I couldn't even figure out what impression I was shooting for, much less how to accomplish it. Which explained why I needed Dylan's help in the first place.

I seemed to have a selection of businesslike and formal clothes, which had been appropriate for loan meetings, church, job interviews and most events with Trevor's moneyed family. Then there were my grungy clothes, which worked for babysitting the twins, making a mess in the kitchen, and watching TV at three in the morning. Didn't I own anything in between—something casual but flattering, something that would draw a man's interest without looking like an obvious attempt?

Apparently not.

No wonder I'd barely had any dates in the past six months, as Amanda so frequently reminded me. I would bet money that *she'd* never had this problem in her life. The woman projected appeal and confidence, and even when she was dressed in ultracasual clothes, her hair and makeup still made her look attractively put together. I'd seen Amanda take fashion risks of mad genius, selecting clothes that made me wince when I saw them at the mall but then drew admiring stares when she wore them in public. I, on the other hand, was just discovering I owned four navy skirts and two pairs of nearly identical low-heeled pumps.

Miriam, you trendsetting daredevil, you.

Cosmetics weren't my forte, either. As one of the bridesmaids in my cousin Beth's wedding last summer, I'd tried to use an eyelash curler for the first time and had almost put my eye out. All right, so I'm a tragic spaz when it comes to girlie tools of grooming, but I'm poetry in motion with an herb mincer. And I'd pit my potato-ricing skills against anyone at the CIA—the Culinary Institute of America, not the group with the spies.

The loud buzz of my nonmelodious doorbell left me with mixed emotions. While I regretted not having changed, at least now I could stop fretting in front of my closet, feeling like an idiot because I had zero idea what to wear.

I turned toward the front of the apartment, pulling out the alligator clip I'd had my hair tucked into and fluffing the liberated locks with my fingers. Perhaps it was for the best that I didn't have time to check my handiwork in a mirror.

Dylan was looking yummier than anything I'd ever cooked, in a pair of gray slacks, a loose-weave midnight-blue sweater and the same leather jacket he'd worn yesterday. A black camcorder bag was slung over one broad shoulder, and in his hand he held a spiral notebook along with—yipes—a copy of *Six Course Seduction.* I ushered him inside thinking that here was someone who had probably *never* felt like an idiot. He had the air of a man who always knew the right thing to say or right tie to wear or right wine to order with a meal. This last analogy reminded me of Trevor the Annoying, but I managed not to grit my teeth as I spoke.

"Hi, your timing's perfect. I just got back from my parents," I told him, omitting my flirtation with wardrobe-induced nervous breakdown.

Dylan set his bag on the sand-colored linoleum long enough to shrug out of his jacket. I breathed in the faint whiff of cologne, inhaling as deeply as if I were judging the aroma of a simmering stock.

"I hope you didn't rush home on my account." His words distracted me from olfactory nirvana.

"Just the opposite, you did me a favor. I love my family dearly, but...have you ever wanted to move far, far away from your relatives?"

He grinned, his green eyes crinkling at the corners in that unfair way that makes men look rugged and sexy, and women just plain old. "Mine live in London."

"Ah." I experienced a spark of kinship over our respective kin. "So you do know the feeling?"

"Intimately." He leaned down to pick up his camcorder, then straightened, raising his eyebrows in question as he hoisted his jacket on a couple of fingers. Maybe he was used to women who had coatracks. And who wouldn't blind themselves with eyelash curlers.

I gestured past the four-by-four foyer and into the living room that made up the front of my place. "You can just throw it on the back of the armchair, if you like. I always toss every—"

My words broke off in horrified silence as I glanced into my mostly tidy living room and realized that a bra lay forgotten and partially wedged between two cranberry-striped sofa pillows. I'd shrugged out of it last night while watching an old television movie with incredibly bad special effects.

I grabbed his arm, propelling him farther into the apartment, toward the kitchen. "You hungry? I'd be happy to whip us up something."

"I wouldn't want to impose."

"Or there's pie," I said, feeling unbelievably grateful to my mother. "Homemade, brought it back from my parents'."

He eyed the container that I'd dropped on the kitchen counter while speeding through my apartment. "I could go for pie."

Great. I'd dish him up some dessert and excuse myself just long enough for a lingerie recon mission.

As he sat on a bar stool on the other side of the kitchen counter, I pulled out a plate. "Want anything to drink with it? Coffee, maybe?"

"Thank you, no. Water will be fine." He smiled. "I'm here to work for you, not the other way around. Unless *you* wanted some coffee…"

Hardly. I felt jittery enough without the full-octane caffeine.

I was en route with a cup of ice from the refrigerator to the filtered faucet on the sink when he announced, "I loved the book, by the way." The cup in my hand made an abrupt detour toward the floor—thank God for plastic. Perhaps "jittery" had been an understatement.

Dylan stood immediately, obviously ready to come around the counter and assist me.

"It's all right," I said, more to appease my tattered pride than to answer any unspoken questions he might have, such as whether or not I always startled this easily. "It wasn't glass. No damage done."

I bent to retrieve the three ice cubes I'd spilled, chunking them in the sink. On the bright side, they didn't bounce off the water spout and boomerang back to hit me in the head. So I had that going for my one remaining shred of dignity.

As he sat down, Dylan observed, "I seem to throw you off. I take it this image consulting wasn't your idea?"

I bit my lip, realizing how little had been my idea lately. What was up with that? The restaurant had been Trevor's, as had the initial cookbook attempt. Breaking up had been his idea, the few dates I'd been on in the last few months had mostly been Amanda's... Outside of the kitchen, where I was ingenious and in control, my last independent, rebellious idea had been to sex up my book.

Hm. Maybe that's why I'd taken a holiday from free-thinking. God knows what I'd come up with next.

"No, it was my publisher's," I confirmed as I opened the utensil drawer and grabbed a fork. "But I certainly recognize the wisdom behind it. You don't have to worry about my being a hostile client or anything."

He grinned. "Hostile isn't how I would describe you. Just a bit unstrung. If it makes you feel better, most people are nervous about being on television or radio. Which provides me great job security, so I quite appreciate it, actually."

I smiled, thinking that I liked this man. Then again, his

occupation was based largely on putting people at ease and teaching others to do the same, so I shouldn't read much into our interactions. "Here." I handed him the plate of pie and glass of water, managing not to do anything as Lucy Ricardo as dump his drink down his front.

"Sorry I don't have any ice cream," I said as he took the first bite. "It's even better à la mode."

He sighed. "No, it's heaven already. You know how often a bachelor in New York City eats something home-cooked?"

"So you—" *Don't have a girlfriend?* As if that was any of my business! "—live in New York? Joan mentioned something about Atlanta."

"Right. Just moved. The weather's far warmer than either England or New York. So far, I love it, but we'll see how I fare during the summer. If I stay that long."

I leaned my elbows on the counter. "Planning to leave already?"

He shrugged one shoulder as he polished off more pie. "Not planning, precisely, but I tend not to sign long leases. I didn't have what you would call a...a settled childhood. I grew accustomed to the moving around."

"So is your family from England originally, or did they move there?" Though his words did come out in an occasionally crisp cadence reminiscent of Britain, he didn't have a native's accent.

"Transplanted from California—I've lived all over. As long as I can generate word of mouth, I can work in almost any city."

"Joan certainly recommended you highly," I said. Gushingly, one might say.

"Great lady. Met her while coaching one of her colleague's bestsellers, and I eventually introduced Joan to her husband."

This information perked me up, for no real rational reason.

He gestured toward me with his fork. "Someone at Hargrave clearly thinks *you* have bestseller potential, and I'm here to help you fulfill it. So, as nice a diversion as it's been to be the center of attention myself, we should focus on you."

Joy.

"Okay, sure. Just, um, let me get something to pull my hair back with so it's not falling in my face while you film me." It was either that or an I-have-to-use-the-bathroom excuse to leave.

I dashed out of the room, making a quick right to retrieve my bra and scan for any other offending undergarments. Then, hoping he was too preoccupied with pie to notice, I hurried past the kitchen/dining room area again to get the clip I'd tossed on my dresser before answering the door. When I moseyed back down the hall, securing my hair in a loose twist as I walked, I found Dylan had rinsed off his plate and unzipped the camcorder case.

"Later, we'll practice your cooking in front of the camera," he said, "but for now why don't we adjourn to the living room? Get comfortable."

That wasn't going to happen, but I nodded anyway. We moved to the other room, and I perched on the edge of my chintz armchair, with all the relaxed ease of a perjurer on the witness stand.

Dylan unfolded a minitripod, then angled his head toward the colorful end table on the other side of the sofa. "Mind if I move this to the center of the room?"

"Go right ahead."

After he'd resituated the piece of furniture, he set the tripod on top of it and positioned his camera to face me.

He flipped open a little side panel that I guessed was a screen and frowned. "You know what? Your sitting on the chair and talking to me behind the camera doesn't make sense. We need more one-on-one interaction to give you practice for dealing with the talk show hosts. Why don't you move to the couch, where we'll be close enough for the camcorder to get both of us?"

Be still my beating heart. "Okeydokey." Had I actually just said okeydokey? Wow, check out the mistress of sophisticated repartee. Too bad silent film was a thing of the past; I'd probably do Hargrave more good on shows that didn't require speaking.

I stood and had made it about halfway to the couch before Dylan straightened, looking pensive.

"Let's talk about your walk first," he suggested.

"My walk?" Hardly an encouraging beginning. "Do I need to put a dictionary on my head for this?"

The corner of his mouth quirked. "No. But straightening your shoulders and smiling would be a good start. You hunch, move with a bit of nothing-to-see-here in your stride. When you walk onto a show's set or into a bookstore, you should *own* the place."

Maybe I could start slowly, with some sort of lease-to-purchase option.

Dylan ran a hand over his wheat-colored hair. "Where do you feel most comfortable, the most in charge?"

That was easy. "Industrial kitchens."

"Right, then. When you enter a room, picture it's the kitchen of a restaurant. Everyone there works for you. You want them to like you, want to inspire their loyalty, but you also want to make it clear you are the boss."

I am the boss. Not Trevor, not Blondie. Me.

I lifted my chin, feeling my shoulders roll back almost automatically. "I can do that." As I retraced my steps to the couch, I had the sense memory of confidence. Even on the first nights of new jobs, I'd rarely doubted myself in the kitchen. And after a few shifts, no one else doubted me, either. They saw Miriam Scott, dedicated chef.

"Perfection."

I sat down on the couch, feeling borderline poised. Until Dylan joined me on said couch, at which point my hormones began to sizzle and zing. I imagined I heard the same popping sound as oil warming on the metal surface of a hot pan.

He was all business, apparently deaf to the little pops. "Later we'll talk about dealing with questions you don't like and how not to give anyone a negative sound bite inadvertently. But my first piece of advice is, when you do these shows, resist the temptation to look at the camera. Unless it's a cooking segment where you're addressing the audience directly, it will make for more natural viewing if you keep your focus on the host. Plus, not staring at the little red light will prevent you from being nervous."

I snorted.

"Perhaps *prevent* was an overstatement," he conceded. "But it should reduce your anxiety, at any rate. So for our little practice session here, keep your eyes on me."

What a hardship.

I dutifully locked gazes with him, my heart rate speeding up. How was I going to answer his mock interview questions intelligently? The way I felt right now, I'd be lucky to form words at all. I nervously wet my lips with my tongue, then froze, realizing he was staring at my mouth. I hoped he hadn't thought I was making some lame attempt at flirting with him. Or is that what I *should* be doing on these interviews?

I couldn't look away, partly because I was once again experiencing that sense of familiarity I'd had last night at the bar—that maybe I'd seen him somewhere before. But mostly, I was immobilized by the urge to shove him back against my couch. Which was understandable, really, considering how long it had been since I'd gone to bed with a man and all the time I'd spent researching supposedly sensual foods.

Dylan swallowed, yanking his gaze downward to consult his notebook. When he glanced up, he wore a polished, benign smile that made me think he was "in character."

"Good morning, Miriam, and thank you for appearing with us today, to talk about your intriguingly racy cookbook, *Six Course Seduction*. It was quite the read, and I imagine the recipes are fabulous, although I personally am hopeless in the kitchen."

I relaxed a little, since I'd addressed this dilemma point blank in the foreword of the book. I suspected he'd used that opening to ease me into the interview. "Not a problem. There are a number of simple recipes that are just elegant or different enough to make your date feel she's worth more trouble than cheese and crackers or delivery food. A caprese salad, for instance, doesn't require much more than slicing, drizzling and the addition of basil, an anciently held aphrodisiac. Almost no previous cooking skills are needed."

He flashed an encouraging smile. "Good. Quick response, concrete example from the book. But make sure your tone doesn't sound too…detached. You want to convey a sense of fun."

If he thought this was my idea of fun, he was insane, but in all fairness, it *was* turning out to be more enjoyable than that college root canal. I returned his smile gamely, determined to do this well. "Another option, if you really don't feel you can handle these recipes on your own, is cooking as a couple, a tactile experience bound to help set the mood. In the early stages of a relationship, it gives you something to do to fill any nervous moments.

"If you're already in the throes of a passionate relationship, working beside one another in a closed space, bumping into each other as you reach for measuring cups and graters...it's all a preliminary tease building toward an unforgettable night. And don't underestimate the aromas. There are some spices that stimulate the senses far more than manufactured aftershaves."

I was surprised at how throaty my voice had become, how convincing my words, since Trevor and I had rarely cooked together. He had considered the kitchen my domain and mostly set foot in it only to try something and offer an opinion. But it wasn't Trevor in my mind's eye now. I couldn't help but imagine Dylan standing alongside the counter with me, his long sleeves rolled up as he reached past me for...no, as he reached for *me*.

I supposed it would be transparent if I suddenly volunteered to whip up something with a lot of basil.

Dylan cleared his throat. "That was great. See, you're hardly going to need my help at all. Next question—do you have a favorite recipe from the book?"

"Um..." Since I was suddenly too distracted to even remember any of the recipes, I just widened my grin and tried to interject a playful note in my voice. "You know how it is—you're in the mood for something one night, but have a craving to try something different the next. All the recipes are good, it just depends on what you're desiring at the moment. Don't be afraid to experiment and surprise yourself with new favorites. You might find yourself wanting something you never expected."

"Right. Good." He swallowed.

"Did you have a favorite?" I asked. "I mean, when you were reading the book was there anything that... sounded particularly delicious?"

Either he had leaned toward me sometime during our question-and-answer session, or I had gravitated in his direction, but as he looked into my eyes, I realized we were much closer together than we had been when he first sat down.

After a moment, he glanced down, presumably at his notes, which were scrawled in a tight, angular script I was surprised anyone could read without a decoder ring. "It was all very, er, enticing. You're really doing quite well with these answers, so we probably don't need to cover all of these tonight."

"You're leaving?" Though I hadn't been looking forward to this exercise, I was looking forward to his absence even less. "But it doesn't make sense for you to drive all the way over here and go so soon."

He lifted his head. "Maybe just a few more... What gave you the idea for the book?"

I blinked. As far as possible comments or inquiries about my book went, this one was pretty innocuous, but for the life of me, I couldn't think of a suitable answer.

My fiancé thought I had all the spicy hotness of vanilla ice cream, and I wanted to prove a point? I sold out because I needed a sensationalized slant the marketing department would approve? I was smashed on wine, and my friend Amanda is a bad influence?

"Miriam?"

"I don't have a reply for that one. Not a good one, anyway."

Was I insane, or did he look relieved by my lack of a response? Hadn't he approved of the last few?

"That's what I'm here for," he assured me. "I doubt your answer is as bad as you think, but even if it is, we'll have it sounding brilliant by the time you do any interviews. So what's the first thing that popped to mind?"

"My fiancé."

Dylan frowned darkly. "I hadn't realized you were engaged."

I loved that he looked bothered by the idea—except he was probably only wondering why it hadn't been mentioned in the personal information he'd been given about me. After all, romance would be an angle we could play up in the publicity pitches. But not even selling a zillion copies would have made another month with Trevor worth it.

"Oh, trust me, I'm not. Anymore. But I was when I initially pitched the cookbook."

"Ah. So the two of you devised the concept together?" He was still scowling.

"On the contrary." I recalled how Trevor had scoffed at the new direction I'd taken. He thought the book would flop spectacularly. That *I* would flop. "He didn't think I had it in me."

"How do you mean?" Dylan looked genuinely perplexed, as if it was puzzling that someone wouldn't look at me and see "provocative author of sexy book." I could have kissed him for that. In my head, I heard *zing! pop!* and the sizzle of steam being released.

If you kiss this man, he will no doubt phone your editor

tomorrow and tell her that you're a lunatic he can't work with. Get a grip.

I told him the truth about Trevor, needing the douse of reality like the splash of cold water. "Let's just say my ex went with a shinier, sexier model." I was like a rugged, industrial kitchen mixer, and he'd gone with something sleeker but less useful. The few times Blondie had been in the kitchen with me, she'd antagonized several of our best kitchen staff. I didn't care how good a cook she was, a real chef knows how to utilize—and motivate—the crew.

"Sexier?" Dylan's gaze slid over my face and down my body, not that he could see much of it beneath the sweatshirt. My body, however, didn't know that and warmed anyway. "So this fellow lacks vision."

"Um..." Unsure how to interpret his remark, I chuckled. "According to the write-ups the restaurant's received, he's full of it. Vision, I mean." Actually, "full of it" was an accurate description of Trevor.

Dylan was still regarding me with such intense focus that my palms became damp and my mouth dry.

"You think I could be sexy?" I wanted to bite off my own tongue as soon as the words were out. "F-for the book tour. You think I can create the right persona?"

His eyebrows shot up, and for a moment, he didn't say anything. "Absolutely. We just need a few practice sessions like this one to get you more comfortable in front of the camera and to develop some good stock answers you can tweak during your interviews. And some appropriate wardrobe selections."

Yipes. "Appropriate isn't code for stilettos and miniskirts, is it? I know that's what most people think is sexy."

He laughed. "No. Just certain colors and outfits with

long, smooth lines for television. Nothing that wrinkles too easily or cuts you off at the waist. Certain styles that might ordinarily look fine on you can be less flattering depending on the camera angles. And considering the tone of your books and the image you want, maybe—"

I found his abrupt halt alarming. "What?"

"It's just a piece of objective advice routinely given to female clients with trim builds, to enhance a camera-friendly silhouette." His expression was sheepish. "A, er, push-up or lightly padded bra."

"Ah." My face flooded with heat. I experienced a moment of dreamlike panic that, if I looked down, I might actually see my unample breasts *shrinking*. "And maybe something low-cut to display the new and improved cleavage?"

"No. As I said, this is simply about body lines and what presents the most photogenic form. I wasn't stating a personal opinion. Er, criticism. You're…"

Of the two of us, he was definitely the more "unstrung" now. I'd moved on to thinking I should've encouraged him to go when he'd given me the opportunity. "I'm sorry, I know I said meeting tonight would be a good idea, but maybe I overestimated my—" *Don't say stamina.* It wasn't a word I wanted to think about with real Dylan sitting next to me on the couch assessing my breasts and fantasy Dylan last seen turning up the heat in my kitchen. "Energy level. I don't think I'm a good subject to work with right now."

He nodded. "Perhaps I'm more knackered than I realized, as well."

Knackered? I assumed from the context that it meant tired, but it wasn't a word I knew. I did know it wasn't the effect I wanted to have on this man.

5

Sometimes, the very contrasting flavors that cause you to think, "Those cannot possibly go together" turn out to be the perfect complements for an unforgettable match.

"YOU DID NOT 'scare him out into the night,'" Amanda protested with a laugh. When it had become painfully clear she wasn't going to quit hounding me for details about working with Dylan, I'd broken down and given her the thumbnail sketch of our evening at my place. "Sounds like it was just late, and the two of you decided to call it quits for the evening."

What I'd decided to call it was a catastrophe, I thought as I nudged salad around on the bone-colored plate.

Showing what a true friend she was, Amanda, who shared my fondness for sleeping until noon, had responded agreeably when I'd phoned at ten this morning and begged her to join me for an early lunch and emergency shopping. Dylan was scheduled to meet me here at the upscale mall later this afternoon, but no way was *he* the person I wanted advising me in Victoria's Secret. I'd never viewed underwear shopping as a team sport, but today I was feeling the uncharacteristic need for moral support.

Amanda jerked her chin toward my side of the small, round bistro table. "You gonna eat that? Lunch was your idea."

My lips twisted as I passed judgment. "This lettuce was probably fresh last week, and they used completely the wrong kind of nuts for this salad."

"Or you aren't hungry because you're nervous about seeing a certain consultant later today," she hypothesized. "Loss of appetite is a classic sign of infatuation."

I deflected the topic from me. "Are all bartenders pseudo-psychologists?"

"Yeah. They teach us about that right after facing all the bills the same way and seeding the tip jar."

Since I had no interest in finishing my lunch and Amanda was already done with her cheeseburger and double order of fries—the government really needed to harness whatever energy source fueled her nonstop metabolism—I reached for my purse. "It's on me. Least I can do for dragging you out while the sun's shining."

"If you really wanna pay, I won't fight you for the bill, but the truth is, I was looking forward to doing some shopping anyway." She grinned. "Some of us actually *enjoy* it, you know."

"Hey, I might, too, if I looked like you. Or had any fashion sense. I was just realizing last night that I don't even like half the clothes in my own closet." Maybe that had been a subconscious perk to being a chef—a uniform that didn't require any thought.

"Well, I didn't want to be the one to say anything…."

"You hate my clothes?"

"*Hate's* a strong word."

I sighed.

"You've never been all that concerned with showing off your assets," she pointed out. "Think about how much work you put into a meal, all that emphasis on presentation. Give yourself the same effort, and you'll have half the guys from here to the Upcountry drooling after you. Sometimes you act like you *want* to be invisible."

Not invisible, exactly, but I had always preferred some degree of privacy and anonymity. I supposed anonymity wasn't going to sell books.

"Okay," I said slowly. "If you were me and you had this tour to do, what would be the first thing you changed? Besides obviously lacking cup size, I mean."

"You aren't lacking, and I doubt Dylan thinks you are either. You know, it's possible he was just uncomfortable with the conversation and that's why he bailed."

"Uncomfortable? He does this for a living."

"Maybe he sees you differently than some of his previous clients." She waggled her eyebrows, in case I wasn't picking up on her hidden meaning.

"Oh, please."

"Well, he had just finished reading your book, right? It's not that far-fetched that he'd be—"

"Amanda. Focus. It *is* that far-fetched, and I legitimately need your help here."

"Fine." The way she grumbled the word made it clear I was ruining her fun. "What was the question again?"

"If you were me, what would you change?"

She brightened. "The hair."

I had to ask? Hers sported a new color and style each season.

"When's Dylan meeting you?" Amanda checked her watch. She had a collection of inexpensive, funky timepieces, and today's was a surprisingly conservative gold-plated chain, but with Disney characters featured on the face. "We might have just enough time."

"For my hair?" I asked nervously. That hadn't been on the agenda.

"Yeah. Thursdays and Sundays are Bruce's days off."

I almost laughed over her knowing her stylist's schedule by heart. The girl took hair seriously. "But if he isn't working today, I'm out of luck, right?"

"Wrong. It's your only shot to be *in* luck. He's sometimes booked months ahead, but I'm willing to bet he'll help you out if he doesn't have pressing plans. First, he adores me. And second, he can't resist a project, no offense. How about I give him a call?"

"Whoa. I thought we were going to shop." I'd planned to get Amanda's opinion on some fashion issues so that when Dylan showed up, I didn't come across as entirely clueless.

The proper way to prepare an amazing scallop ceviche? *That* I knew. The history of saffron? You betcha. What differentiated this year's neckline from last year's? Not a clue.

Amanda waved her hand. "The shopping center is available all the time. Bruce, not so much. His place is just off 17, and if we can get you back in time to meet Dylan, it will be the best spent couple of hours since I dated Lars Cavanaugh—whew, the things that boy could do. Just let me make a quick phone call to see if I can set it up, okay?"

I wasn't even sure yet what we were trying to set up specifically, but I nodded anyway. *You wimp.* Hadn't I been thinking as recently as last night that I needed to regain control? Then again, I had actively sought out Amanda's help, knowing that this was more her area of expertise than mine.

Now I just had to deal with what I'd set in motion.

"YOU LIKE IT, don't you?" Amanda asked with a self-satisfied smile.

"Of *course* she likes it." Behind me, Bruce pursed his lips, his image reflected back at me from the mirror at his personal station. There'd been quite the stir when he'd arrived to put the empty chair to use. "Why wouldn't she? I did it after all."

Considering he'd agreed to come in on one of the few days he turned his salon over to the stylists working for him, and considering he'd done a hell of a job, he was allowed a little presumption.

I could admit now that I'd had my doubts. Before I'd been seated, they'd asked me to change out of my top and into something that looked like it came from the Hefty Garbage Bag Couture Line. During past haircuts, I'd worn a drape over my shirt, but no one had actually taken my clothes from me to reduce the chances of my trying to escape. Then Bruce had suggested short, which I'd protested. I don't care how "in" wispy layers are, I don't want strands falling in my eyes or sticking to my forehead while I'm cooking. And then there had been the foil he'd wound through my hair until I began to understand how a Thanksgiving turkey must feel, all sealed up in aluminum.

But it had been worth it.

"It looks amazing," I admitted. "I couldn't visualize how it would turn out, but it's perfect."

My hair still wasn't exactly blond or exactly brown, but it was warm and shiny now, not flat. Caramel-colored, with scattered streaks of gold. And it wasn't shoulder-length anymore. Bruce had cut it at a reverse angle, so that it was slightly longer in the front, tapering past my chin and framing my face. Though the overall style was shorter, I'd still be able to pull it back without strands escaping.

"Amanda's right to call you a genius," I added, figuring it couldn't hurt to score her brownie points since she'd arranged this for me. The outcome had definitely been worth sitting still, holding my neck at the specified angles and enduring the acrid smells of various hair chemicals, which had been a pungent reminder not to take for granted the sautéing garlic and onion *I* got to work with.

He spun the chair around so that I could stand up and go exchange the waterproof salon wrap I wore for the shirt I'd hung up in a small dressing room. I put my own clothes back on, frowning at the drab oatmeal color of my sweater. But then I ran a hand over my softer-than-ever hair and smiled. I'd planned to buy new clothes, anyway, and now I could make wardrobe choices that complemented my new look.

I walked back out and found Bruce at the front, running the credit card I'd given him. "Thank you."

He winked at me. "For a friend of Amanda's, anything. But promise me you won't stop with the hair. The new you cries out for eyeliner and lipstick. And I wouldn't shed actual tears if you burned that top."

Burn was a little extreme. Just because it wasn't an exciting shade didn't mean that crewnecks weren't classic staples. It was January, after all, and a body needed to stay warm. I glanced toward Amanda, noting the sleek black ribbed turtleneck that clung to her with dramatic allure. Then again, perhaps I could find a more flattering way not to freeze to death.

"We have to get a move on if you're going to be on

time for Dylan," she said, eyeing me with proud joy. "He'll flip when he gets a look at you!"

"You think he'll like it?" Even though I knew the style and highlighting were dramatic improvements, I still experienced a moment of shyness. Should I have included my image consultant on major decisions about my appearance?

"Like?" Bruce scowled at me. "You are now a creation of Bruce. He will love it."

I signed my receipt, managing not to chuckle until Amanda and I were out in the parking lot. "He's gifted with hair, but you have to admit, Bruce takes some getting used to."

"That style of yours is what I'm trying to get used to," she said as she climbed into the passenger side of my car. We'd left hers at the shopping center. "You look like an entirely different person."

When I was younger, I'd assumed longer hair would help me look more feminine, downplaying what I'd considered a boyish build, but Bruce had worked magic, highlighting surprisingly pretty facial features. Surprising to me, at any rate. If Dylan and I hadn't had an appointment to meet, it might have been fun to buzz by Spicy Seas to see what the kitchen crew thought. And if Trevor just happened to end up ruing the fact he'd ever let me go, that wouldn't suck. As mildly entertaining as the daydream was, though, Trevor and his opinion had stopped being all that important to me. I was free to move on to other romantic attachments.

But an attachment with a man so accustomed to polished sophistication that he made his living at improving it? A man who looked like walking perfection and lived in another state? Granted, Atlanta wasn't all that far away, but Dylan had said himself he had nomadic tendencies.

Nope. Dylan Kincaid, the man who had been sent to work with me on a professional basis and might be of the opinion that my breasts were too small, was a temporary fixture in my life. No haircut could change that—not even one by Bruce.

AMANDA BEGAN DRIFTING AWAY from me as soon as we walked inside the shopping center. Well, maybe less *drifting* than dashing. "Have a great afternoon! Give Dylan my best. Or better yet, give him yours."

"It's not like you have to sprint off," I tried to tell the would-be matchmaker. But by the time I finished the sentence, she was little more than a distant blur with a cartoon puff of smoke trailing after her.

I was on my own—at least until I spotted Dylan standing outside the large department store where we'd agreed to meet. My breath quickened, and my step momentarily faltered, but I managed to get to the large planter he was leaning against without hyperventilating or twisting an ankle. He hadn't noticed me yet. He was watching a couple of cute kids chase each other around, or possibly the willowy redhead trailing after them.

When he caught a glimpse of me in his peripheral vision, he did a gratifying double take. The small fortune Bruce had charged to my card had been entirely worth it. "Miriam. Wow."

I grinned. "You like the hair?"

"I like. A lot. When did…who…it's different."

I stopped, crossing my arms over my midsection. "But good different, right? I can quit worrying that I let him cut it too short or that it's not a camera-friendly color or something? Amanda took me to see her hairdresser."

"Amanda?" Dylan was still staring, looking somewhat dazed. He may have been the first man ever to have temporarily forgotten her after being introduced. I kind of loved him for that.

Who would have thought I would ever hold a guy so enthralled he blanked on meeting my gorgeous best friend? "Really pretty bartender," I supplied. "You met her the other night."

"Oh. Uh-huh." He blinked. "Well, we should be getting to work, shouldn't we?"

Probably, but the back-to-business suggestion was deflating. "I'm ready as I'll ever be. Go easy on me."

He chuckled. "Most women don't consider shopping painful."

Ha! Showed what he knew about standing in a fitting room during bathing-suit season, hoping that pale white skin was making an anti-melanoma fashion comeback.

"Maybe it won't be so bad," he added. "I've actually been told I'm an enjoyable companion."

That I could believe. "It's just that this doesn't rate high on my list of top-five ways to spend an afternoon." I fell in step with him as we entered the store, involuntarily tensed for the moment a saleswoman descended upon us.

"What do you do for fun?" he asked. "Besides cook."

I grinned. "Eat. Number-one favorite pastime, hands down. I'm also a big fan of eclectic late-night television—everything from specials on the History Channel about Greek philosophers to classic black-and-white sitcoms to mind-rotting, low-budget movies that revolve around cheesy acting and zero plot." Food and

TV—could I have sounded any more like the original prototype for the couch potato? I quickly added, "And I love racquetball, although convincing Amanda she has time to go with me can be difficult. I obviously don't play with Trevor anymore."

"Trevor? He's the idiot ex?"

I nodded, giving Dylan points for use of the term *idiot*. "What about you? Hobbies?"

He looked startled by the question, as if he hadn't expected reciprocal conversation. I supposed many of his clients were more interested in solving their immediate problems than learning about him. "I like to travel, which I believe I've already mentioned. And I'm an avid reader. I'm also a fan of soccer—watching, not playing."

"Hi." A flawlessly put-together brunette inserted herself in our path with a broad smile. "Is there anything special I can help you with today?"

I expected Dylan to return her smile and accept her offer, with explanations that I needed a whole new wardrobe and perhaps some lighter fluid for my current one.

But he merely shook his head, rebuffing her with a friendly, "No, thank you."

She looked disappointed in a way I doubted had anything to do with commission and moved on to the next people entering the store, casting one final glance over her shoulder in Dylan's direction.

I raised my eyebrows, surprised he hadn't pointed at me with a grimly determined, *Your mission, should you choose to accept it…* "You're not calling in the cavalry? I half figured today would be like that scene in *Pretty Woman* with multiple people bringing me whole racks of clothes to try on."

He grinned. "Well, first of all, I should point out that you'll have to buy your own clothes, but if you can afford whole racks, more power to you. Mostly, though, I didn't get the impression you'd want a team of people lining up outside your dressing room. If I was wrong, we could call her back."

"No, you weren't wrong." The fewer people standing around discussing what my flaws were and how best to minimize them, the less likely I would return home wanting to stick my head in the oven. "I'm not really one for crowds."

He studied me for a minute, then shook his head. "That's fine for today, but I am being paid in part to get you ready for those packed book signings full of adoring fans."

I thought he had unrealistically high expectations, but one could always hope. Fans meant sales, and if I were to interview at other restaurants, maybe a successful book would give me a little cachet. "So…what first?" *Please don't say bras.*

He ran his gaze from my head to toes, then back again, slowing on the return trip. Did he have any idea that my pulse was accelerating in direct inverse proportion? "Color. I realize I haven't known you long, but you seem to lean toward darker colors like navy or neutral tones like gray or beige. If you prefer dark, black is one choice, but I think some warmer shades might work nicely. And a few monochromatic outfits will help lengthen you on television.

"Not," he was quick to add, "that I think you're short, just that the camera—"

"Right. Lines, I got it." And I did. He was trying to help me, and I should cooperate, not be sarcastic or defensive.

I turned toward a rack of blouses and blazers, scanning the available hues. But the clothes were…stuffy. I could tell because they closely resembled a number of the ensembles I already owned. "These are awful, aren't they?"

"I wouldn't go that far," he said diplomatically, "but I think we can do better."

"Maybe *you* can, but I'm terrible at this stuff," I admitted.

"Follow me, then." He led me toward a rack of sweater separates. The first thing he picked up was a chocolate-brown knit tank top with very thin straps.

It would be a lot more revealing than anything I'd worn in front of him so far, and even though I knew it was silly, I swallowed nervously as though he'd just asked me to model a lace teddy. "A little chilly for January, maybe."

He held up a matching sweater. "That's why you'd purchase this, too. But you'll be surprised at how hot it can get under the studio lights in a small television station. Mind if I ask what size you are?"

I answered, realizing the day would go quicker if he could help me look for what I needed, and silently offered up a prayer of gratitude for every mile I'd ever jogged and abdominal crunch I'd performed.

He handed me two pieces that should fit, and my fingers brushed his, a phantom spark igniting between us. For a moment, he stilled, gazing at me with an intensity that was neither impersonal nor businesslike. When a woman pushing a stroller banged into the rack from the other side, we both jumped.

There was something strangely intimate about having Dylan dress me—and it grew increasingly difficult not to fantasize about his *un*dressing me. I tried to recall whether or not Trevor had ever taken an interest in what I wore or gifted me with apparel of any kind, but his presents had always been of the kitchen-appliance variety. While I loved cooking gadgets, the hindsight suspicion that he'd only ever wanted me for Spicy Seas' benefit made his gestures less thoughtful.

Finally, I began to stagger under the weight of fabrics I was carrying. Dylan was still adding skirts and scarves to his half of the Miriam Scott Winter Collection. I'd be worried about paying for this if I weren't already convinced a lot of it would look ridiculous on me. He'd just picked up a red dress—had I ever worn anything red?

"I think we should get a room," I told him.

His gaze snapped toward me. "Excuse me?"

"We should go ahead and find a salesperson to unlock a dressing room if I'm going to try on all of this before the summer stock arrives."

A few moments later, a woman with dollar signs in her eyes was unlocking one of the booths that lined the back wall. Inside, a fancy antique replica chair sat opposite the gilt-framed mirror. Outside, Dylan settled himself onto a less ornate seat, giving me instructions to show him any selection that I didn't categorically hate beyond all reason. Though it was stupid with the door now closed between us, I felt exposed as I slid out of my pants and pulled my sweater over my head.

He could see my arms lift up in the air above the door, my calves beneath it. *So what? Your forearms aren't exactly X-rated territory.* And he likely had better things to look at on the sales floor than the occasional glimpse of flashed limb. I was probably only dwelling on Dylan because I didn't want to put on these clothes and scrutinize my own reflection. Yeah, that was it.

Since it was one of the last things he'd picked up and therefore on top of the pile, I grabbed the red dress first. I could get it out of the way, explain politely that I hated it and move on to a more sensible selection. The garment had straps, but also long sleeves, baring a substantial wedge of each shoulder. With the cut-out style and bright color, I'd expected to feel cheesy, like someone trying too hard to be sexy. But it made me feel surprisingly feminine. Maybe it was just the lighting or the new hair color, but I felt as if I had a slight glow, a radiance that hadn't been there before. Could be a wisely placed trick mirror, but I was willing to give the dress the benefit of the doubt.

I smoothed the fabric into place, running my hand over the tapering waistline. The skirt was simple, falling to an unremarkable length that wasn't long but also wouldn't leave me freezing this time of year. The real focus of the dress was definitely the neckline and sleeves, and I had to admit, they looked good on me.

"You're not going to believe this," I started to say as I reached for the door handle.

Dylan sat up straight in the chair he'd been lounging in, his eyebrows shooting up. "Nice. What's not to believe?"

"I thought it would look ridiculous."

"Hey! I selected that. You don't trust that I'm qualified at my job?"

"Sorry. But I don't know many guys whose specialty is making women look good." In fact, Trevor only seemed to care about women making *him* look good.

He grinned. "I've made it a point to get to know a lot of women. Really well, in fact. Maybe I should have included studying them under 'hobbies.'"

My skin warmed, and I suspected the rosy glow created from the dress and department store lighting now had biological help. As of today, I could tell Amanda with absolute certainty that my image consultant was not the stereotype she'd first expected.

His smile suddenly became less rakish and more conspiratorial. "Then again, it could also have something to do with my mother being in the fashion industry and my absorbing the knowledge through environmental osmosis. But it's nice to take credit for it myself."

I returned to the dressing room, relieved by his qualifier since it stopped me from thinking about how closely he'd been scrutinizing me and wondering how I measured up to all those other women he'd "gotten to know." I tried on several other pieces, including the chocolate-brown sweater set, although Dylan shook his head at it, declaring that it didn't make me look half as smashing as I deserved.

"We should find long jackets for you," he said through the door as I was changing into a skirt and diagonally cut sweater.

For a moment, the disembodied voice gave me a jolt of recognition. Did Dylan sound like someone else I knew? No one came to mind, although I was certain that voice was familiar.

Then he spoke again. "And some low-rise pants that accentuate your hips."

I opened the door, chuckling. "That would be easier if I had hips, don't you think?"

His eyes captured mine. "Oh, trust me. You do." The simple sincerity with which he spoke made me feel more alluring than any of the outfits I'd tried on…or anything Trevor had ever said to me.

"Th-thanks."

"Don't mention it." He nodded his approval at the outfit. "Just doing my job, as they say."

Was this why Dylan was such a successful image consultant, because he didn't convince you to project a certain appearance so much as get you to see yourself a different way? He was damned good at it. There had been moments today when I'd felt genuinely sexy.

Don't read anything into it. You heard the man—this is what he does for a living. He's here to bolster your confidence so you can speak on cable television without falling apart.

I finally worked my way through the seemingly interminable pile of clothes we'd collected, deciding on the dress and an off-center sweater and skirt. The ensemble had looked too funky on the hanger, like something better suited to Amanda, but once I'd put it on, I hadn't needed Dylan to explain that the cut added intriguing angles to my figure. I'd always worn slightly baggy clothes to hide what I'd considered my boxy appearance, but all I'd done was make myself look like a minimonolith.

There were a couple of "maybes" in our selections, but Dylan pointed out that there were plenty more stores we could visit before I handed over money for something I didn't love.

"That's the part of the job that took me the longest to adjust to," he said as we strolled out of the store. "It's very easy to spend other people's money, piling up things you think they should have without taking into consideration their pocketbooks. And I'm a bit spoiled in that regard myself."

I glanced at him. "You grew up with money?"

Rather than answer, he reached for the garment bag I had hanging from one hand over my shoulder. "Want me to carry that for you?"

"It's all right. This is nothing compared to some of the things I've had to haul across a kitchen. Heck, this can't even give me second-degree burns."

He laughed. "Well, you do have very toned arms. Great shoulders."

There was that rosy glow again. Too bad I hadn't met Dylan last month—I could've led Santa's sleigh if Rudolph had wanted the night off. I didn't thank him again, not wanting him to ruin the compliment by pointing out he was only doing his job. It was all objective, like an inspection: nicely rounded shoulders, breasts need help, carburetor in good shape, could use new shocks.

"How hungry are you? Do we shop more, then have a late dinner?" he asked. "Or should we eat now to build up energy for round two?"

Under different circumstances, that could have been a very sexy question. "I wouldn't say no to food." I ran through a list of the restaurants in the shopping center and what they each served. We picked a casual eatery where we shouldn't have to wait long for our orders.

Dylan followed me in the door, and I told the hostess two for nonsmoking, then waited as she checked the chart in front of her, tapping my toes to an old rock hit playing through the speaker above. As I began to hum along with the words, I had a flash of déjà vu and recalled the first night I'd met Dylan, when I thought he'd looked remarkably familiar for someone I was sure I hadn't met before.

I turned so suddenly I almost lost my balance. "Wait a minute, I know who you are!"

6

Another way to use the ingredients listed here is a blindfolded taste test—spoon-feed your partner a few sweets, then shake things up with something spicier. Surprises are a surefire way to keep things lively.

WITH THE STRONG RESEMBLANCE and same last name, the only reason I hadn't made the connection sooner was that seventies rock star J. D. Kincaid had been more or less before my time.

Dylan was tense, his face uncharacteristically grim as he waited for me to follow up on my spontaneous declaration.

"You're J.D.—"

"Yes. I think our table's ready." He glanced past me, pointedly toward the hostess, who led us to a freshly cleaned booth.

Bizarre. I was about to have dinner with the son of a bona fide celebrity, two celebs actually. Thanks to cable television "rockumentaries" I'd seen, I knew that Kincaid had married an almost-supermodel in the seventies and they'd had a son. J.D.'s biggest hits later came out at the turn of the decade, but despite a few popular singles, his career hadn't taken off in the eighties. I could remember my older brother, during his blessedly short-lived electric-guitar phase, trying to learn a few of the songs from J.D.'s one bestselling album.

To my knowledge, J.D. had never had another successful record, though he and his wife had been able to milk their combined fame for all it was worth. They were both the types who showed up in cameo roles in random movies when I was growing up or on the celebrity versions of game shows. At some point, they'd moved to Europe, but while they'd mostly dropped out of America's public eye, I felt sure anyone passing through the shopping center today could name at least one J. D. Kincaid song, even if the singer were more likely to be found now on a cable where-are-they-now special than the top of the charts.

I glanced across the table. "That first night I met you, when I asked if we'd met—"

"Right," Dylan said flatly. "I get that sometimes. Been told I look just like him."

"I wouldn't say that, exactly." There were differences, but enough similarities that anyone who had seen J.D.'s picture would do a double take, even if they couldn't quite recall who Dylan reminded them of. Now that I did remember, I had to say I thought Dylan was even better looking than his sex-symbol father. For one thing, years of wild living didn't show on his face.

I suppressed the urge to pry, wondering if the tabloids had exaggerated that wild living. For the sake of the child Dylan had been, I hoped so. Then again, even if all the stories had been manufactured, it couldn't have been easy growing up with cross-continental rumors. And I thought *I'd* had it bad because my parents occasionally drew attention to themselves or, worse, me. Dylan must have started despising outside notice at an early age—witness his not telling me when I first mentioned his looking familiar, and his obvious discomfort now.

His laugh was on the sardonic side. "Aren't you going to ask about him? Or Kiki?"

"The fashion model." I remembered what he'd said earlier in the department store. "So, she's who taught you so much about clothes and what flatters women's bodies?"

"I learned some about clothes through listening to her and people she worked with." His smile became more genuine. "Women's bodies I figured out on my own."

Yowza. I wouldn't mind being a study subject.

The waitress's delivery of our water glasses was well timed, and I immediately reached for the cool drink in front of me. Meanwhile, Dylan fielded the woman's question about whether or not we wanted an appetizer, telling her that chips and salsa would hold us over until our meals came. She went to get the tortilla chips, and as we perused the menus, the subject of his parents faded away. I could tell he didn't want to talk about them, which was fine with me. If there was one thing I prided myself on, it was an un-Scott-like ability to respect privacy.

I set my menu aside, having decided on their spicy shrimp pasta dish. "I'm glad you suggested eating now. I'm hungrier than I realized. Trying on clothes can really take it out of you."

He lowered his own menu, his eyes unreadable for a moment. "I wouldn't know about that. All I had to do was sit back and enjoy."

A ripple of warmth went through my midsection at the implied pleasure in his tone. Had he really enjoyed this afternoon? I wouldn't have blamed him if he'd said watching me model clothes had grown so tedious he'd considered gnawing off his own arm to escape—*I* would have been bored senseless, were our situations reversed.

My gaze trailed down over his shoulders and chest. Okay, maybe not. Having him parade different outfits would have given me a great excuse to look at him, and seeing his bare arms and calves on the other side of that thin door…

He spoke, his voice causing me to jump like a guilty kid caught with her hand in the cookie jar. "This is the first time a menu has ever made me self-conscious."

"Hm?"

"I keep thinking about your book."

"Book?" My mind was still on the cookies.

"Your writing really stuck with me, and now that I'm reading the descriptions of the dishes here, ingredients you detailed are jumping out. I feel like a man on a date insisting that he's only ordering the oysters because he really likes them." He glanced up. "Not that we're on a date."

"I knew what you meant." The hasty reminder that there was nothing romantic between us would have been disheartening if I weren't so preoccupied by the notion of *Dylan* being self-conscious. It was like being told the world was flat and the whole round thing had been a government conspiracy. "Don't let the aphrodisiac hype make you feel conspicuous—sometimes a mushroom is just a mushroom."

He laughed, the warm husky sound all the aphrodisiac any red-blooded woman would ever need. "I have to say, you're not what I expected when Joan asked me to take on this assignment."

"Really." It wasn't entirely a question, since I wasn't

sure I wanted to know the specifics of how I didn't meet his expectations, but he answered anyway.

"A lot of my clients get nervous because they take themselves too seriously. Some are actually so into themselves or whatever message they have to impart that they border on obnoxious, in which case it's my job to tone them down for the public. But you aren't like that."

"Thanks." As compliments went, "you're not obnoxious" wasn't exactly swoon-worthy, but it was a hell of a lot better than "you *are* obnoxious." "Toward the end of my relationship with Trevor, I guess I was starting to feel too serious."

The unintended personal admission startled me, but Dylan didn't seem to notice my surprise. "Too serious about the relationship?"

"No, just in general. Trevor likes to be the life of the party, and that sort of relegated me to 'straight man.'" He was the one who dreamed things up, I was the one who worried about the details. He was the one who laughed with our friends in the living room, while I checked on the hors d'oeuvres in the kitchen—not that I minded cooking instead of hearing his same jokes for the tenth time. "I suppose it doesn't matter. Even on my own, I'm essentially quiet and reserved."

Dylan's eyebrows rose. "Reserved? Did you *read* your section on human desserts?"

I felt heat climbing in my face. "Um. Well, you can't believe everything in print."

"Pity," he murmured, his gaze locked with mine. "But speaking as your media consultant, I wouldn't use that as an interview answer. Let them wonder."

The way I was wondering now? Trying valiantly not to picture Dylan with a cherry on top, so to speak.

Bless the heaven-sent waitress who interrupted our

conversation—and my distinctly unangelic thoughts—by arriving with the chips and salsa. "Bet you all were feeling forgotten," she said apologetically. "We have a big party in the back, with separate checks and constantly changing minds about who wants what. Sorry about the delay."

"Not a problem," I assured her. I would have been happy to see her even if she'd spilled the salsa down the front of my shirt. According to Bruce, I could've used the splash of color anyway.

My newfound luck held out when Dylan reached for the tricolor chips. Eating would forestall further comments on anything I may have written while under the influence of post-breakup bravado.

Dylan dragged his chip through the small black plastic *molcajete* full of salsa, scooping up a healthy amount of the three-pepper sauce. But his eyes widened, watering ever so slightly, as he swallowed.

He grabbed his water glass, taking two large gulps before saying, "Wow. If I'd known they made it this hot, I would have started with a smaller amount."

"You don't like it?" I asked, gearing up to make my own evaluation of the restaurant's house salsa.

"More that I wasn't prepared for it." He dunked a second chip and ate it without any noticeable smoke coming out of his ears. "See, it's fine if you know what's coming. Either that, or I burned off all my taste buds the first time around."

I laughed, then popped my own chip into my mouth. "Hm." I was unimpressed.

Dylan raised his eyebrows as he echoed my question, making it more of a statement. "You don't like it."

"I've had better." I'd *made* better, but I didn't want to toss myself in that category of obnoxious clients he'd mentioned earlier. "Clearly, we're not dealing with people who appreciate subtlety. I don't care how trendy it's gotten, cilantro should be handled with a delicate touch. And spicy is about more than—I'm being unbelievably annoying, aren't I?"

He grinned. "I thought it was a bit endearing, actually. This is my first time out to eat with a chef. Enlighten me."

No one had to ask me twice to talk about food. "I like to catch people off guard with my recipes. Unexpected pairings, flavors that blend in a unique way. Food that has a delayed kick. *Anybody* can load up a salsa with enough jalapeños to make your throat burn, but I'm after taste, not acid indigestion.

"In my opinion, there are two kinds of hot. The painfully obvious, which, as you pointed out, burns a layer of nerve endings off your tongue and is the flavor equivalent of a busty blonde in spandex and stilettos. Then there's the less instantaneous but secretly more daring kind of hot, like wasabi, which looks cool and unassuming, but burns all the way down and all the way up to your sinuses. The flavor equivalent of…"

I didn't really have a good example for that one, and besides, I was sounding entirely too zealous about what was essentially mushed tomatoes and some spices. Borderline lunatic dictator. *Not enough cumin? To the Bastille with him!* If I'd shown this degree of passion for Trevor, we'd probably still be together.

In retrospect, it was tough to recall how I'd managed *any* passion.

"Well." I cleared my throat. "You get the picture."

Dylan was regarding me intently. At first, I assumed he was trying to figure out an inoffensive way of suggesting therapy, but after a moment, I realized there was a heat in his expression that might not have anything to do with the jalapeños. Answering warmth tingled in my face and, more pleasantly, throughout my body. The man had such amazing, clear green eyes that it seemed the most natural thing in the world to be staring into them, lost. As if we were the only two people in the world.

"*Miriam!* Ohmigosh, is that you, sweetie? Look at your hair!"

I about launched out of my seat, making a mental correction. *Three* people in the world—me, Dylan and my sister-in-law, who was barreling toward us.

As I blinked my surroundings back into focus, I saw that Eric and a couple I hadn't met followed a few steps behind Carrie. I could hide under the booth, but considering there was no tablecloth, I'd just look silly down there.

Dylan cocked his head to the side. "Friends of yours?"

"Family." If the word came out sounding as though we should make the sign of the cross to attempt warding them off, it wasn't deliberate.

"Girl, your hair looks just fabulous." Carrie slid onto the bench next to me, beaming, while the other three stood awkwardly beside the table, like a mariachi band who'd forgotten their instruments. "Doesn't it, Eric?"

"Fabulous," he echoed dutifully.

I would have made introductions, but Carrie didn't give me enough time. She whipped her head around to give Dylan an appreciative once-over. "Is this your TV guy? You said you two would be doing some shopping, but you didn't tell me he was such a cutie. This is the guy who's going to get her all ready for her big interviews," she told the couple with my brother. Then she glanced back to me for confirmation. "Isn't it? Oh, dear. I didn't interrupt a date, did I? Please don't tell me I've horned in on one of the few dates you've been on since Trevor."

"No," Dylan interrupted, once again making the public service announcement that our evening in no way resembled a date. "You were right the first time—TV guy."

"Or, as it says on his business cards, my image and media consultant," I put in, sounding admirably cheerful for someone with so "few dates," who would clearly die alone and surrounded by cats. "Dylan Kincaid, this is my sister-in-law, Carrie Scott, my brother, Eric, and…"

"Our friends Michelle and Dan Halloway," Carrie supplied. She nudged me with her elbow. "Michelle's the one with the single brother I told you about, if you're interested. Just look how cute she is—they come from a very attractive family."

"Thanks, but I can get my own dates." I wonder if the clenched teeth made me seem defensive? Because I wasn't. I was totally unbothered by my loving relatives suggesting in front of Dylan that I needed help finding men.

"So you're the one who wrote that book?" Dan asked me. "Carrie showed it to us back at the house. I'll never look at an avocado the same way."

"Er, thanks."

"Is it true what you wrote about pomegranates increasing fertility?" Michelle asked, her expression hopeful. "Because we've been having trouble getting pregnant."

"Dan's got slow swimmers," Carrie said sympathetically.

In my peripheral vision, I saw Dylan blink. My own

expression felt frozen. If I'd been Dan, my head probably would have exploded on the spot, but no one in their foursome looked surprised at Carrie's announcement. For that matter, after knowing her six years, it's a wonder I still get surprised.

Michelle reached across my sister-in-law to pat my arm. "Oh, I know what you're probably thinking, but don't worry. When you've been trying to conceive, you end up having all kinds of conversations you never expected. We stopped being shy about it months ago."

Good for her. Meanwhile, *I* had been sitting here, minding my own business, lusting after my dinner companion, and now I was hearing about some total stranger's sperm count? Or speed. Or navigational skills. Whatever.

"I think the pomegranate lore is more mythology than science," I told her, "but I guess it couldn't hurt to try. And, uh, good luck?" I wasn't sure the right thing to say under the circumstances. *Sorry about your boys, Dan?*

"Hey," Eric said, hopefully about to change the subject and not offer any advice such as choice conception positions. I didn't need to know any intimate specifics about how my nieces had been brought into this world.

My brother did redirect the topic, staring across the table at Dylan. "We haven't met before, have we? You look really familiar."

I swung a concerned glance in Dylan's direction, remembering his strained expression when I figured out who he was, but when our eyes met, it looked as if he were fighting a grin.

All he said was "I get that a lot."

Carrie engulfed me suddenly with one of her enthusiastic hugs—the kind I normally brace myself for first.

If she weren't so sweet-natured, the woman could have a serious career in the WWF. "It was terrific bumping into you, but we should dash. We've been doing the tourist thing here today with Michelle and Dan, and your mom agreed to keep the girls while we squeezed in an early dinner and a movie. I hate missing the previews."

"Absolutely, you should hurry!" The shopping center boasted a sixteen-screen, stadium-seating theater, and as far as I was concerned, Carrie et al couldn't get there fast enough.

Once she'd stood, Eric leaned down to give me a quick, brotherly peck on the cheek and to mutter with a discretion I hadn't realized he possessed, "Forget Michelle's brother. You and the television guy look cozy enough."

I kept my voice equally low. "It's not like that. And you say one thing to embarrass me, there will never again be a freshly baked cream-cheese pound cake on your birthday!"

He chuckled under his breath. "Embarrass you? You mean say something like, 'What are your intentions toward my baby sister,' or 'So, have you kids tried out that naughty recipe on page forty-six yet?'"

I started to smack him on the arm, but decided that would probably invite questions about our brief whispered conversation. Then I smacked him anyway, offering a dry, "Mosquito," by way of explanation. Granted, it would have been more believable if we'd been outside. And if it weren't the dead of winter.

Before anyone could point this out, however, our waitress arrived, speeding along their goodbyes by politely shooing the Fearsome Foursome out of her way to set down hot entrées. I was *so* tipping this woman.

Once Dylan and I were safely a few bites into our respective meals, and the memory of the encounter was fading some—mainly because I psychologically repress emotional trauma—I risked glancing over at him. He was grinning broadly, although every few seconds, he made a valiant effort to stop.

"Glad to provide the entertainment," I muttered.

"I was just recalling all those times I wished I had a brother or sister," he said. "Thanks, I believe I'm cured now."

His good-natured tone cajoled a smile out of me. "I love my family, but they can be…vivid. You should see Carrie and Eric when they're with my parents."

"Don't worry, I'm all too familiar with 'vivid.'" There was an expectant silence, as if he realized he'd just opened the door for questions about a past he didn't want to discuss and was waiting to see whether or not I walked through it.

I took a big conversational step backward. "So, how's your fish?"

"I don't have your discerning palate, of course, but it's pretty good. Speaking of food…we should get together for more filming, this time of you in the kitchen," he said. "I'm sure cooking is second nature to you, but cooking photogenically—with a camera in mind—can be a little different. So can cooking *with* someone."

I laughed. "I probably talk sometimes like I'm a lone artist, me and my emulsified sauces against the world, but the truth is, it's a group effort. I'm used to working with a sizable kitchen crew bustling around."

"A trained kitchen crew, though, not some morning-show ham getting in your way and distracting you with banter. That's what you should practice—cooking alongside a culinary neophyte."

"You mean like you?" If he could say I wasn't photogenic, I could call him a neophyte.

He considered this. "Probably not. It would work better if I'm free to man the camera and offer directorial suggestions. I don't suppose you have many friends that don't know their way around a stove? Or maybe someone in your family..."

Someone in my family? I'd be swilling the cooking wine within the first five minutes. "I'll call Amanda and see if there's a time she's free to help us. She makes possibly the best drinks in the country, but the girl can't cook."

"Perfect."

If he said so. Amanda was definitely one of the few friends I had who was clueless in the kitchen, but today she'd seemed too interested in what role Dylan could play in my life besides just professional consultant. Would she drop any hints in front of him? While she was nowhere near as prone to over-sharing as my family, nothing about male and female relationships made her shy. There had been occasions in the past when she'd decided it was necessary to give me a less than subtle nudge.

I'd just have to take my chances, I decided with a covert glance across the table. Without Amanda, it would be Dylan and me alone in that small kitchen, enveloped in heat from the stove and tantalizing aromas as I talked him through various preparations, perhaps even reached over to show him what I'd meant. There would be touching. And definite lusting.

It was possible I could appeal to Amanda's sense of compassion and get her to stow any sly remarks or knowing glances for the day. But if not, nothing she said would be as embarrassing as catapulting myself at Dylan.

7

Your kitchen says a lot about you—you want an inviting atmosphere, tidy but not devoid of personality. Keep cabinets stocked so you're equally prepared for simple but satisfying quickies, or more complicated adventures the two of you can take your time to enjoy.

I EXHALED A LABORED PUFF, hoisting more department-store bags than one person should ever be carrying at a time—and it was still fewer than Dylan held for me as he accompanied me to the main exit. Unreal. "Until tonight, I thought 'shop till you drop' was just an expression."

He chuckled. "Be proud of what you accomplished. You now have the basics for an entirely new wardrobe, even beyond your book publicity. And everything we picked up at that going-out-of-business sale was practically a steal."

Good thing he was in favor of stealing because there was a chance I'd have to knock over a bank or two to pay off my credit card. But we *had* found some amazing bargains. Besides, with the exception of the occasional kitchen supply, how often did I splurge on myself? Part of me might even have found it a little bit…fun. My companion had had a lot to do with that, smiling appreciatively at me for most of the evening and not expressing impatience a single time as I'd weighed different options and what they would cost me.

I had no prior experience with all-day clothes shopping, but Trevor had hustled me out of cutlery stores in exasperation more than once. He liked things to happen now—which was why, when he'd tried to "share the workload" by making a snap decision about suppliers, we'd ended up having to break the contract and find a new seafood vendor a short while later. Dylan had been great. Funny, charming, quick to offer his opinion, but not pushing me when I disagreed.

Recalling my original fears about what my consultant would be like, I muttered, "You would never have forced a woman into poofy hair."

His eyebrows shot up. "Pardon?"

"Nothing." I preceded him outside, sighing in pleasure over the refreshing briskness of the cool night. Mall air starts to feel recycled and unnaturally flat after a few hours. "Where are you parked?"

"Way over on the other side. But with it being dark out already and all of this—" He lifted the bags with a grin. "I figured I'd walk you to your car. I'd tell you I was brought up to be a gentleman, but if you read even one tabloid that came out in the eighties, you wouldn't believe me."

"The media hype everything, though, right?" I hadn't really meant to ask, but Dylan had brought up the subject. And I was curious about his childhood... mostly because I was curious about the man himself and events that might have shaped him.

He laughed wryly at my question. "The media might exaggerate, but not nearly as much as my father. He strived to create that persona, then lived off it for two decades. I was raised to believe image is everything."

"Is that how you got started in this line of work?" I asked, deciding his parents' motto had clearly left an impression.

"In a roundabout way. My upbringing gave me unique insight into creating or reinventing a public image. How others see us can be really important, but a lot of people never live up to their potential. Why not use my knowledge to help them?" He grinned. "Especially since it pays so well."

We'd reached my car, and I shuffled my bags around, trying to free up a hand to unlock the trunk.

About the time I'd decided it would be easier just to set them on the concrete, Dylan said, "Here, I've got them."

Somehow he managed to hold everything while I popped up the lid. When I turned to take part of the load, he was already leaning forward to put the purchases in the car. My breathing quickened at his nearness, and I forgot to grab any of the bags. He brushed past me, pausing for a moment, before setting down the last of the stuff. Had he felt that spark, too? Or was he just wondering what in the heck was wrong with me?

He straightened. "Well, that's everything." His smile warmed me despite the breeze swirling around us.

The wind blew a lock of hair across my cheek, and Dylan surprised me by reaching out to brush it back. His fingers were warm against my skin, rougher than I might have guessed, but not in a bad way. His touch sent a sizzle through me, all the way to my toes. Dylan's eyes had grown heavy-lidded, and he seemed to subtly sway toward me as though he, too, felt the pull of the moment.

My heart beat an erratic rhythm. Was I crazy for thinking he might kiss me?

Apparently so, because a moment later he dropped his hand. He simultaneously lowered his eyes, and I wondered if he was deliberately avoiding my gaze.

When he spoke again, he sounded nonchalant and businesslike. "So, you'll call me to let me know if that practice cooking segment with your friend is a go?"

I nodded, feeling too confused to form words. Maybe the desire I thought I'd seen in his expression had been a trick of the parking lots lights. Or maybe my new haircut was more powerful than I thought, and Dylan had momentarily been overcome with lust for me. I rolled my eyes inwardly at the idea, then decided that whatever he had been feeling, it was probably for the best that nothing had happened. I didn't normally make out with men I'd only known a few days, and my one experience mixing business and romance hadn't turned out so well.

I rocked back on my heels. "Thank you again for all your help today."

"Don't mention it." He gave me an encouraging grin. "This is just the beginning of a whole new you."

MY FIRST LIVE TELEVISION appearance was less than a week away. Probably anyone in my position would be suffering from a massive double whammy of dread and performance anxiety. Except that my particular case of nerves had nothing to do with next week and everything to do with the fact that Dylan would be at my apartment in less than an hour! And I still couldn't decide between the aphrodisiac-laced omelet or the fruit empanadas—perfect as a seductive dessert, morning-after breakfast *or* midnight snack when you finally realize you're famished for something other than each other.

Amanda was sitting on the edge of my kitchen

counter, watching me spiral toward the edge of sanity. "Is there something I could do to help, maybe phone in a prescription for a heavy tranquilizer?"

"Tranquilizer?" I stopped my manic opening and closing of cabinets. I had been pulling out ingredients for three dishes—the glazed melon I had decided on and the two unconfirmed potentials—I'd also been doing subconscious inventory to see what I had on hand and whether or not I should be considering another, as yet unthought of, recipe. "I'm not that bad."

My claim was so patently unbelievable that Amanda didn't even bother refuting it with anything other than sardonically raised eyebrows.

I sighed, sagging against the pantry door for support. "All right, so I'm a little nervous about this whole cooking on television thing." Nigella Lawson had nothing to fear from me in the way of job competition.

"*That's* what you're so antsy about? Television?"

"Do you really find it so hard to believe?"

"Fine." She shook her head. "Treat me like I'm an idiot instead of your best friend. But if it makes you feel any better, you look fabulous today, and I'm sure certain consultants who don't make you antsy will think so, too."

I wasn't trying to shut her out, but my burgeoning attraction to Dylan verged on ridiculous. I barely wanted to admit it to *myself*—not that any woman wouldn't understand why I found him appealing. Or why I discreetly drooled from time to time. But the flutter I got in my stomach when he was around came from more than just raw lust. I hadn't known the man long, but I knew I liked the way he treated me, his easy humor and admiration for my ideas. He frequently praised the book, and if we hadn't had to leave the shopping center Thursday night due to their hours of operation, I probably would have ended up bouncing some ideas off him for the second book Hargrave was expecting.

That is, if I could talk to him about food as foreplay without getting distracted by raw lust.

Since I wasn't comfortable articulating any of that, however, I just flashed a grateful smile for Amanda's compliment on my appearance. "Thanks for the confidence booster." I'd been afraid that my hair would pull that treacherous stunt where, two days after you leave the salon, you can't duplicate what the stylist did and you look like an escapee from electroshock therapy, but so far, so good.

"You're welcome—and I wasn't just blowing sunshine up your skirt. If we were the same size, I'd be begging to borrow that top from you sometime."

Wow. Amanda coveting my clothes? But it wasn't as if I could take sole credit for my *Pygmalion*-like improvements. Well, *Pygmalion*-like if Henry Higgins had been trying to transform Eliza into a risqué "foodie" personality instead of a proper lady.

Today I was wearing chocolate-colored jeans that, if not tight, were definitely more body-hugging than most of the pants I chose and a colorful chenille scoop neck Dylan had persuaded me to buy. He had said that anything ending right at my waist didn't show my figure to its best advantage, and during our spree, I'd come to realize how longer tailored tops worked for me. But he'd further insisted shorter ones could work, too, so here I was in a sweater that would flash a little midriff as I moved.

Hey, I was the one who did all those freakin' crunches—might as well show the occasional glimpse of abs, right?

"When this is all said and done," I told Amanda, "I'll *buy* you a sweater since I feel like I'm asking you for a favor every time you turn around!" It was Saturday afternoon, and I was sure there were a zillion other things Amanda would rather be doing after a hectic Friday shift and before the busy one she was certain to have tonight.

"Nah, it's nice to feel needed for a change. Just think about all the times you've been there for me in an emergency."

I stared at her blankly. Amanda wasn't what I considered emergency-prone.

"That broken-condom incident over the summer?" she said. "You were the one who weathered the pregnancy scare with me."

True, but "the scare" had been sitting in stone silence in her living room for three minutes as we waited to see whether or not the stick came up with two lines or one. When there had only been one, she'd murmured a heartfelt prayer of gratitude and had never mentioned it again.

"And what about that time last year," she continued, "when Bruce was in Portugal on vacation, but I was determined to get my hair done before the holidays? You bought me a hat while I waited for him to get back and fix the neon orange that other idiot caused."

I laughed at the reminder. The baseball cap had read What Did I Ever Do to Anger the Good-Hair Gods?

I'd never realized how comfortably low maintenance our friendship was, but if Amanda was grateful for three minutes out of my life and a cap, then she sure wasn't asking much. Normally, I was equally undemanding, but lately everything seemed off-kilter—even before Dylan's arrival. The more I'd thought about the book that was coming out, the more I'd questioned how it fit into who I thought I was. Or who Trevor thought I was, or my family. I suppose it would be the height of bad cliché to say I felt like a butterfly finally emerging from its cocoon—ready to make its wormy ex eat his heart out.

Not that this was about Trevor. He hadn't even seen the new cut or clothes, so he certainly wasn't the motivation behind them. It was just that when he'd laughed at my ravamped cookbook idea, I had barely stopped myself from agreeing with him. At times, the thought of me promoting a flirty book full of sensual pictures and double entendres *did* seem silly. But why should it? I had as much sass as the next…sassy person. And that was the point I wanted to make, to myself, first and foremost.

I wished Trevor and Blondie all the happiness in the world; they deserved each other. Hell, I hoped he asked her to marry him. I happened to know of a cookbook that would make an excellent shower gift—although my gracious and forgiving nature would prevent me from attaching sticky notes telling the bride-to-be that, for her sake, she should pay particular attention to recipes reputed to improve a man's stamina.

"Miriam?" Amanda asked after I'd been silent a moment. "Still trying to decide what to make? Keep in mind, you don't want to lose the newbies."

I nodded. Dylan had already given me similar advice, warning me to stay away from complicated dishes or fancy equipment most people wouldn't have in their kitchens. We wanted the book to appear accessible, not intimidating. "Eggs it is. Those are hard to screw up."

She snorted. "You've never tried sunny-side up at my house. But I'm game for anything, especially if you're going to feed me. I'm starving."

I raised my eyebrows. "You're kidding." Since I'd been feeling restless all morning, I'd baked a batch of lemon poppy-seed muffins, many of which Amanda had scarfed down as soon as she'd arrived. She may have also raided my refrigerator for other goodies while I was finishing my makeup application. I had actual mascara on my uncurled lashes.

"Where do you put it all?" I demanded.

Her cheeks flushed with color. "Well, some people eat when they get..."

"What?" When she didn't answer, my gaze dropped involuntarily to her flat abdomen. "There hasn't been another broken condom!"

For a second, she looked stunned, then burst into laughter. "Good grief, no. That would require having sex."

"Has it really been that long? That's not—" I cut myself off from saying "that's not like you" when I realized it would probably sound unintentionally insulting. It wasn't as if she were a card-carrying player of bedroom bingo, just that there had never been a shortage of attracted and eager guys. For that matter, I knew of several who would probably sacrifice a limb to get her number now. "There's no one you're interested in?"

The blush in her cheeks intensified. "I never said that. He's just different—"

"*He,* as in a specific yet somehow conveniently unspecified guy whom you completely neglected to mention the other day?" I couldn't believe she'd been holding out on me! Or that I was so wounded she'd kept the secret.

She grinned unrepentantly. "Well, there wasn't a lot of time to talk about him, what with all my heckling you about Dylan."

"Which you can put a stop to any second now. I work with him, and he'll be gone in a week or so. There's nothing more to it."

The doorbell croaked out a greeting, and my heart leaped to my throat.

My friend slid off the counter with a dry smile. "Yeah, I can see by your expression how he doesn't get you worked up at all. You want me to answer the door?"

"No." I defiantly raised my chin. I could show her I wasn't rattled. Or, I could at least leave the room before I gave her any more ammunition for teasing me.

Dylan stood on the outdoor welcome mat, looking casually sexy in jeans, a long sleeved T-shirt and a disarming grin. "Hi."

I swallowed and invited him in. "Dylan, you remember my friend Amanda White?"

He nodded, flashing that grin her way. Too bad. It would have been fun to pretend the smile was just for me, but Dylan was charming with everyone. It meant nothing. "Thanks for your assistance. Miriam tells me you're as bad a cook as I am."

Amanda laughed, but without any hint of flirtation, as if she were unaware the room had suddenly gone five degrees warmer upon his arrival. "Glad I could help," she said. "You guys just tell me what you need, and don't say I didn't warn you when the smoke alarm goes off."

I glanced back at Dylan, having taken just enough of a break that it couldn't be considered staring. "How much of the cooking do you want me to delegate?"

"Whatever it takes to give the host camera-friendly busywork. They'll want to be involved, even if they don't know a teapot from a toaster oven, but if they botch something up, they make your recipes look harder. So provide them with something simple to do, and keep the more impressive maneuvers for yourself."

"Got it."

Amanda followed me into the kitchen, but Dylan remained in the dining room half, setting his camcorder up on the dividing counter. There were no windows in the kitchen, so despite the sunny day outside, I had already flipped the lights on to better illuminate the room. I glanced around quickly, trying to see it through Dylan's eyes. The gas range, navy countertop and the sparkling clean but slightly cluttered assortment of small appliances. I stayed away from personalized aprons or cutesy mugs, but hanging on the back wall, next to the pantry, there was a large heart-shaped spice rack my dad had made for me. On the back were the words Love Is the Spice of Life. I realized Dylan had already seen all of this, but his visit seemed more personal this time. I was cooking for him.

Yeah, *cooking,* I reminded myself. It wasn't as if I were performing a striptease. One, Amanda was in the room. Two, there are just some places you don't want hot substances splattered. I mean, not even the Naked Chef is really naked.

Dylan eyed the assorted supplies I had lined up on the counter. "Wow, how much were you planning to cook? You know these are short segments, right?"

I began moving aside the dough ingredients for the vetoed empanadas. "Amanda and I were just brainstorming before you got here. But I've decided on the melon in rosemary syrup and an omelet."

"Omelets are sexy?" He grinned boyishly. "Should we warn Denny's?"

I smirked. "You're hilarious. Maybe you should have your own show."

He shook his head. "Nah, I'm a strictly behind-the-scenes guy. You, on the other hand, we are going to make a star. Ready to get started?"

I set a heavy skillet on the stove, then shoved a white cutting board toward Amanda. "Omelets have a lot going for them as far as couple food. If you've already made love, it makes a great breakfast in bed." I was proud of myself for discussing sex in a cool, even tone, and hoped Amanda was taking note of my unrattled state.

Whether my friend was impressed or not, I couldn't say, but Dylan had some suggestions for improvement. "Miriam, when you do this on television, you want to occasionally look toward the camera instead of addressing the stove burners."

Picky, picky. I took a deep breath and looked up. "Sorry. Is this better?"

"Much." His eyes met mine, and I tried not to shiver.

"All right. As I was saying, omelets are a great morning-after meal. Or even a protein boost to refuel mid-marathon. And if you're still working toward the starting line, you have your choice of sexy ingredients to use for filling, including different cheeses, spices and—"

A chirping sound interrupted what I was saying, and Dylan and I both swung our gazes to Amanda.

"Sorry," she muttered, reaching into her pocket to retrieve a silver cell phone that was only two sizes up from being a good Barbie doll accessory. Amanda unfolded it in thirds, then tapped something on the screen. "Hello?"

Was I wrong, or did she sound…anxious? Almost a

little breathless, as if she'd had to run down a flight of stairs to answer instead of simply pulling the space-age phone out of her slacks.

Wanting to do something other than ogle Dylan, I began grating Gruyère cheese. It gave my hands something to do while I shamelessly eavesdropped on Amanda's conversation, a feat she was making more difficult by progressively lowering her voice. I gave a little start as I realized my actions were similar to what my mother would be doing under the same circumstances—except Mom would interrupt to ask Amanda to speak up.

"Now?" Amanda asked in hush tones. "N-no, I'm thrilled that you called. I just…" There was a pause and I suspected she was looking my way. But since my attention was focused on cheese and in no way on my friend's private conversation, it was hard to be sure. "Let me call you right back, okay?"

There was a little beep as she disconnected the impressive piece of Skipper technology. "Miriam? I know the plan was to help you out today, but…"

It had been The Guy, whoever the heck he was. Her flustered manner was so obvious—and so un-Amanda-like—that I was sure even Dylan realized it had been a man on the other end of that call. I didn't know who this mysterious object of affection was, but he was clearly important to my best friend. And I'd be a self-absorbed twit to shame her into staying.

"We'll manage fine without you—right, Dylan?"

He nodded easily. "You're actually helping me make a point about flexibility. You'd be stunned at the technical problems that pop up in studios or the number of stores that won't have the books in stock when Miriam shows up for a scheduled signing. So we'll call this practicing for plan B."

"Thanks, guys. Miriam, I'll call you later, 'kay?"

"You'd better," I teased, feeling pretty out of the loop.

Absolved of guilt and duty, she strode toward the front door, calling out, "You two don't do anything I wouldn't do." Except that the wicked way she'd drawled her prohibition made it clear the field of activity was still wide open.

8

You don't have to pull out all the stops the first time you cook for your sweetie. The best scenario is to leave him wanting more….

DYLAN GRINNED at Amanda's enthusiastic retreat. "New boyfriend?"

"I guess. Haven't actually met him." Or, technically, known about his existence until today. "In fact, I was just teasing her earlier this week about how slow her dating life has been lately."

As soon as I'd said the words, I wished I could take them back. Would he remember how Carrie had said the same thing about me the other night?

I gestured weakly after my friend, wanting to keep focus away from me. "Amanda's great. Whoever this guy is, he's lucky."

"You two are pretty close?"

"Yeah." I might even have been taking that a little for granted until recently.

"You're lucky to have such a good friend." His tone bordered on wistful for a second, which surprised me. He struck me as far too engaging ever to be lonely.

"Does moving around make it difficult to stay in touch with your friends?" I asked, telling myself it was none of my business but undeniably curious about him.

After a moment, he smiled and shook his head. "I'm used to it, and there are trade-offs. Like constantly getting to meet new people from different walks of life, and never being anywhere long enough to get tired of it."

Dylan came around the counter. "Well, looks like it's just you and me. Ready to get cooking?"

"Sure." I reached above the countertop to pull down a saucepan. "I can work on the omelet, if you want to mix up the rosemary syrup for the honeydew. A very simple, but sensual dish."

"Because of the rumored properties of rosemary, right?" He took the pan from me. "See, I've been doing my homework."

I laughed at his boyishly self-satisfied expression. "Well, yeah. Rosemary's pretty fragrant and has been considered a stimulant for ages, but I'm more concerned with the overall tactile experience than specific lore. Don't get me wrong, aphrodisiacs make a nice touch for the book, but they aren't how I pick the recipes. For instance, roses are symbols of love, and some people recommend a salad tossed with rose petals as a good first course for setting the mood. Personally, I don't see any strapping guy at my table getting all that hot over eating flowers."

Dylan grinned. "Have to agree with that...there are definitely sexier uses for rose petals."

My breath caught. Tantalized by the question of just how and where Dylan would use them, I thought maybe I'd been too quick to rule out the Naked Chef concept. Especially if I could have had a Naked Assistant. "R-right. But, whether or not melons are known to have sensual properties, it's hard to go wrong with a dish you can describe as sweet, firm, juicy or...you get the idea."

"Quite." He nodded for emphasis. "Melon, sexy. I'll make a note."

"I know some really good cantaloupe dishes, too," I blurted, scooting back and wincing when I hit the knob of the silverware drawer.

He set the pan down and reached for me. "Miriam, I know you're nervous about these interviews, but it'll be fine. You just need to relax."

Apparently under the misguided notion that it would help relax me, Dylan had started kneading my shoulder with his right hand. Ripples of sensation slid through me—warm, heady and delicious. He moved his hand slightly behind my head and massaged the base of my neck, his fingers now playing against my bare skin rather than the soft knit of my sweater.

"Mmm." Had I just *purred?* Embarrassed to have made a noise that sounded like something from my neighbor Mrs. Asher's manically friendly cat, I quickly opened my eyes. Banishing feline tendencies from my voice, I shot for a lighthearted tone. "So does Hargrave pay you extra for masseur services?"

He dropped his hand. "Sorry, perhaps I shouldn't have done that. I'm always trying new techniques with clients, to see what works. I'm sure cooking is like that, too."

"Yeah. Just like that." I moved away, toward the cutting board I'd pulled out for Amanda earlier. I suddenly felt like chopping. A lot.

Despite the tension I felt, once I was issuing instructions and we were focused on individual preparations, the practice session went well. For one thing, Dylan seemed to be genuinely enjoying himself, which brought a smile to my face.

"This is actually kind of fun," he said as he reached

a finger to his lips and licked off a drop of honey. "Sticky, but fun."

I rolled one ingredient-filled omelet into thirds with my spatula. "Technically speaking, I don't encourage people on my staff to lick their hands while we're working, but since I don't expect the health department to show up here, we should be okay."

He leaned toward me from the other side of the stove. "That smells incredible."

A flush of feminine satisfaction blossomed through me. Work, I reminded myself. He saw me as a "client." "So, how do you think I'm doing television-wise? Any more pointers?" He'd been making suggestions throughout our working together.

"Just superficial tips."

I almost laughed. Which part of projecting a rehearsed persona *wasn't* superficial?

"Such as rest the night before," he said. "And it never hurts to have a facial a few days before a televised appearance."

I put *improve skin* on the to-do list right under *buy more flattering bra,* not that I resented the tip. The thought of my pores on someone's big screen was enough to send me shrieking toward the nearest day spa.

"Check."

Dylan flashed an approving grin. "I expect you'll be wildly successful and make me look great. You know your stuff pretty well, and if you can talk *me* through making something, you'll be fine with any host who gets underfoot. The good ones should know enough to back off and let you do your job. Just don't be surprised if they want to refilm a few shots or get some sound bites after everything is said and done and you thought you were finished."

"No problem." In fact, whether it was my increased confidence caused by my new-and-improved appearance, practice directing Dylan through the recipes today or sheer self-delusion, I was starting to look forward to the television segments.

I glanced toward the syrup he'd finished. "That needs to cool. Let's get it in the refrigerator while I whip up the other omelet, then we can eat."

We finished in an atmosphere of companionable triumph, me feeling secure that I could hold my own on *Good Morning Westbridge,* Dylan proud of himself for preparing a small side dish. Granted, his preparation wasn't going to earn him a James Beard Award, but that was the cool thing about food—it didn't have to be complicated to be damn good.

"You really *don't* cook much, do you?" I asked him as I whisked eggs.

He shrugged. "Until now, I thought it was a viable lifestyle choice. I come from a long line of non-cooks."

I thought about pictures I'd seen of his glamorous mother and his touring father. "So was there a housekeeper or someone who made you soup when you were sick?"

"I guess. We had some staff that changed depending on where we were living or how annoying the tabloids were. For the most part, my father didn't mind the publicity, even of the negative variety, because he figured when you were a rock star, that couldn't hurt sales. But when Kiki's dress size made it to a tabloid during a year when she wasn't feeling in top form, she fired everyone and started from scratch."

"Huh." A far cry from *my* mother, who would confess to people in the store's candy aisle that she probably shouldn't buy junk food because she was thirty-six pounds overweight. Then she'd shrug, say life was short and buy the food anyway. "Was it difficult being in the limelight like that?" Camaraderie had begun to envelop the kitchen along with the scents of rosemary and tarragon, making my inquiries about his childhood feel completely normal.

"No, my parents loved it." He leaned against the counter, fidgeting with the bowl of sliced melon. "At least, they did when they weren't worried about being a size larger than was flattering."

"I meant was it difficult for *you*."

He blinked. "But I was never in the limelight. I hardly saw them during school terms, and at the places I attended, I didn't stand out. Other students came from far more visible families. The media certainly didn't bother with me. I ruined the party image they liked to cast of my parents. Maybe if I'd been an illegitimate love child, *that* would have been news."

I laughed dutifully at the joke, but the matter-of-fact way he'd described his upbringing bothered me. I was relieved he hadn't been milling around some debauched mansion while rocker friends of his parents threw wild parties—hey, I've seen some of the grittier episodes of *Behind The Music*—but I now had a mental picture of Dylan tucked away in some drafty boys' school, forgotten and neglected, while his parents enjoyed their famous lives.

Maybe I should rethink watching so much late-night cable.

The man had obviously turned out all...right. My gaze slid over his body as I made the assessment, and somehow my concern for him became something less platonic. If I had to guess, I'd say it happened about the time he bent to pull the syrup off the bottom shelf of my crowded fridge.

Nice butt.

Dylan straightened and glanced over his shoulder, probably to ask me about final preparations for the melon now that our syrup had cooled. Instead he merely raised his eyebrows in surprise.

"I should apologize," I stammered. "For, um, staring."

He came toward me, and my body tensed into a humming state of electric stillness. As he reached past me to set down the cold dish, I started to expel my breath, thinking he'd only been approaching the counter. I'd just happened to be in the way.

But now both of his hands were free, and he hadn't moved away. "Don't apologize on my account. I didn't mind the turnabout. After all, I did plenty of staring the other day at the shopping center."

He leaned forward, his eyes bright with seductive intensity, his face only a breath from mine. *He's going to kiss me!* That hadn't happened much since Trevor and I had ended things. There had been a few perfunctory good-night kisses at the end of unrepeated dates, and one, more amorous embrace from a guy who'd wanted to see me again. Perhaps if kissing him hadn't been wetter than hurricane season on the coast, I would have considered it.

Instinct told me kissing Dylan would be sublime, possibly to a nerve-racking extent. "You can't really count that as staring," I babbled. "During the shopping, I mean."

His index finger gently traced the edge of my bottom lip, and my knees threatened to buckle.

"Because you were just doing your job, right?" I'd never considered myself an anxious rambler, but then, most men didn't make me nervous. I was normally just calm, capable Miriam. In Dylan's arms, I was—

No longer *in* Dylan's arms.

He'd dropped his hands to his sides. "My job. Of course. I..." He trailed off, his gaze still on my lips.

"So, um, no more advice then?" I had a little suggestion for myself: learn when to shut up!

"I—your mouth...teeth!" He snapped his fingers, looking relieved. "A lot of people like to have them whitened before any camera close-ups, and you can do that at home by yourself. No need for costly professional appointments if it's not a priority."

I smiled weakly. "I'll keep that in mind."

Who in their right mind had let me publish a sensual book? Here I'd had a hot, charismatic guy cornering me in my own kitchen, obviously thinking about going in for the lip-lock, and because I'd pointed out that we were supposed to be working together, the conversation had digressed into possible stains on tooth enamel. Sheesh.

On the bright side, the incident gave me an idea for my next book—a section on mood-killers. To keep it all food related, I'd probably talk about the heartbreak of onion breath and pitfalls like that. Maybe a few reminders about mints and other suggestions would keep others from standing frustrated and unkissed while humiliation cramped their bellies.

My appetite was DOA, but it would have looked odd if I refused to eat my own cooking, so I managed a few bites of egg once we were seated in the dining room. The food fell to the pit of my stomach with a dull thud, though I made a point of praising Dylan's efforts.

As soon as I could do so without seeming too much like someone hell-bent on getting out of an awkward situation, I asked, "So, are we all done here? Because I was planning to run by Spicy Seas and pick up my check. I've been so preoccupied with other things this week, and I should duck in before they get busy with an early dinner crowd."

He pushed away his empty plate, an expression of keen interest on his face. "You mind company? I've been wanting to see this restaurant of yours."

This was news to me, and also a major wrench in my "Escape! Flee!" plan. After all of Dylan's patience and suggestions, could I refuse without seeming churlish? I didn't want it to sound as though I didn't want him to come with me because he didn't kiss me.

"Sure. The more, the merrier."

He stood, helping to clear dishes with a smile. "I don't usually think of that as applying to only two people."

That was okay. I'd been lying about the merry part.

WALKING THROUGH THE FRONT DOOR of Spicy Seas filled me with conflicting feelings. It was like coming home… after the person you'd been living with had kicked you out and changed the locks. Though I hadn't been gone long, this vacation was the only time I'd ever taken away from the restaurant since Trevor and I first chose the location. Normally I was enveloped with a sense of belonging when I walked inside, but today I felt like someone seeing the place for the first time. The front area was mostly polished wood surfaces—the hostess podium, hardwood floor, wall paneling and benches for patrons waiting to be seated. To add personality and color in the entrance, we'd hung a painted sign featuring the redheaded mermaid with the playful smile Trevor and I had picked for our restaurant's logo. Today, she looked vaguely as if she were laughing at me.

She never would have let a man she wanted get away just as he'd been about to kiss her.

"Hey, long time no see!" Regina Carpenter was the hostess on duty. It had been only five days since we'd seen each other, but even that felt unnaturally long, considering it wasn't unusual for me to spend sixty hours a week here. She beamed at me, then her gaze swung to Dylan, her eyes filled with appreciation and curiosity. "Table for two, is it?"

I shook my head. "We just ate, actually. I came by to grab my check and see if there's anything I need to address. Paperwork, or questions, or vendor problems or…anything?" Hopefully, she knew that "or anything" was my way of asking how the restaurant had been running in my absence, without putting her directly on the spot.

Dylan seemed to get the hint that I wanted to talk to my friend, so he walked farther into the restaurant, peering around the partial front wall to look into the dining room. I saw it all clearly in my mind's eye—the tables spaced out among slim columns and bright seascape paintings beneath lazily circling fans. Each table was enlivened by a vivid blue cloth and a dainty yellow vase of flowers. I missed this place, yet didn't feel I belonged the way I once had.

"You look great," Regina said in an awed whisper. "And *he*'s amazing. New boyfriend?"

She sounded so thrilled for me, I half wanted to lie, but I shook my head. "No."

"Too bad. Trevor would go through the roof. He will anyway, when he sees you. He's in his office. And you-know-who is in the kitchen." Big eye-roll from Regina. "There was another hullabaloo in the kitchen last night, and Jojo said he was quitting if *she* ever messed with your recipes again. She wanted to add her 'personal signature,' but I don't think the customers were happy with the so-called improvements. She blamed complaints on 'the incompetent staff.'" Regina glanced around guiltily to make sure her boss didn't catch her ratting on his girlfriend.

I was torn between indignation for my crew and a less-than-noble satisfaction that Blondie's "improvements" hadn't been well received. I applauded a chef's creative drive, but she should come up with her own dishes, instead of tinkering with mine. And calling my staff incompetent? She was darn lucky they didn't shove her in the meat locker, not that they would have left her there. Long.

"Thanks for keeping me posted, Regina."

"No problem...but you didn't hear it from me!"

I winked at her. "Hear what?"

Joining Dylan, I cast a glance around the main dining area, where a few groups of people were having late lunches. Lively music played through the speakers above, but at a low enough volume not to overwhelm conversation.

"Well, what do you think?" I wanted to know.

He pursed his lips. "Not bad, but I imagine it's the food that makes it special."

"Miriam?" Trevor's shocked tone was loud in the uncrowded dining room.

I turned toward him, forcing a gracious smile. I wasn't going to charge in here on the defensive, sounding threatened about Blondie's changes in the kitchen. But I remained where I was, letting him come to me. The closer he got, the more his hazel eyes widened.

"You look..." He trailed off, casting a sidelong glance in Dylan's direction, and his expression cooled. "Different." He managed to make it neither a compliment nor something directly offensive.

"I am," I said simply. "Trevor, this is Dylan Kincaid. Dylan, Trevor Baines."

"Ah, the one you told me about?" There was a faint note of disdain that Dylan lessened with a polite smile.

I blinked in admiration as he served Trevor's passive-aggressive manner right back at him, only with more refinement. I knew image-conscious Trevor was going nuts, wondering what I'd said to other people about him.

"Did you need something, Miriam?" Obviously sensing Dylan was a foe he didn't want to take on, Trevor turned back to me. Wise move.

"My check, for starters. And I thought maybe there were some things we should discuss."

"In my office, then?" His gaze shifted back and forth as if he feared I'd make some kind of scene in the dining room. Odd, since if I'd been the type to make scenes, maybe I would have been "exciting" enough for Trevor. Not that I wanted him back at all. Somehow, his handsomeness had kept me from noticing before that there was something vaguely rodent-like about him, how beady his hazel eyes could get as they darted around.

I looked up at Dylan, feeling he'd been subjected to Trevor long enough and that, frankly, any further interaction wouldn't paint me in a flattering light, since I'd been the one to date the guy for so long. I pointed toward the small bar on the side of the room. "Would you mind—"

"Not at all, love." He suddenly sounded terribly British in an appealing James Bond kind of way, and I noticed Trevor stiffen at the endearment. "I'll be waiting for you."

I shot him an adoring smile in gratitude for the way he was handling meeting the jerk who had dumped me. I know it's a petty emotion and I should be above what Trevor thought, but there's still something deeply gratifying about a gorgeous man flirting with you in front of the guy who didn't appreciate you.

Once Dylan had strolled toward the bar, where I was sure my friend Lewis would give him whatever he wanted on the house, I followed Trevor into the familiar office. It smelled like his cologne, and my nose crinkled at the scent. Pleasant enough, I supposed, but a little overbearing. And not very original. It was one of those popular sprays you were likely to smell on any third guy who got on an elevator with you.

I took a seat in one of the taupe leather chairs, waiting for Trevor to unlock his desk and pull out my check.

He spun the key ring around in his fingers, his eyes narrowing in a reproachful expression. "So, who's the guy?"

"Dylan Kincaid. I believe we covered that outside."

"Is he in the business?" Meaning restaurant, of course.

"Nope. I do have other interests, you know." Not that I had any reason to believe Dylan shared my fascination for grade-B horror movies or racquetball matches, but that wasn't any of Trevor's concern.

"Have you let him read that book?" Trevor asked. "Because I worry about you, what people will think when it comes out."

I rolled my eyes. "Much as I appreciate the concern, I'm sure it will be fine."

He was shaking his head, continuing as if I hadn't spoken. "People will get the wrong impression. They don't understand how timid you really are."

"Timid?" I had been laid-back, sure. Unconcerned with flashy appearances, absolutely. But I'd been extremely competitive in cooking school and authoritative at work. I'd never been timid. Well, except maybe today when Dylan had almost kissed me.

I hated not having kissed him. *So go for it.* I straightened in my chair, considering the rebellious idea. Why not? My book was a subtle—all right, not so subtle—text on going after what you wanted. If Dylan was what I wanted, what was stopping me from acting?

"Okay, not timid. Reserved. Which can be very classy in a woman. I thought maybe I needed someone more like me, but the truth is—"

"Trevor, you did me a favor when you broke up with me. We're completely wrong for each other."

He frowned, and the Poor Baby face slid over his features like a snug mask. "That's just the hurt talking. I suppose I deserve your reluctance. I realize now I didn't properly appreciate you. But deep down, you know we make a good team."

I held back a bark of laughter. Blondie must be working out worse than Regina had suggested. I thought about Dylan's observation, that it was the food that no doubt made the restaurant special. Trevor was trying to appear his normal, cocky self, but there were new lines of worry etched around his eyes. He was concerned I wouldn't come back, but he wasn't admitting it, as he blathered on about our romantic destiny.

"I think this time apart has been good for us. For me, anyway, it was a real eye-opener." Even his attempt to sound chastised came off as arrogant. He actually thought he could have me back? As if I'd been pining for him to come to his senses for six months? "I've realized what I almost lost."

"Not almost. Did."

He waved his hand dismissively. "I screwed up, but I can make it up to you. The real you. You're not one of these brash women with a sailor's mouth like that bartender friend of yours."

"Amanda?" The friend who had tried to tell me *before* the breakup that Trevor might be all wrong for me?

"Or some chatty housewife with no sense of decorum like—"

"If you're about to say my sister-in-law, you should stop before I smack you in the face with something. I know how particular you are about your looks." Carrie might not be perfect, but she was a good person and worth ten of Trevor. I stood, wanting to get my money and get out of here. The past five minutes had been more time than I'd ever hoped to spend alone with him from here on out.

Which could make coming back to work difficult. *So don't.* Who was this rebellious new inner voice...and where had she been all my life?

It would have been gloriously satisfying to tell him then and there that I quit, but I decided to wait until after I'd finished my paid vacation. I'd earned it. After putting up with this guy, I'd practically earned a medal...or a visit to a good therapist to have my head examined. How had I ever mistaken that our meshing well in a business partnership somehow translated to a good romantic pairing?

"Miriam, you're not—"

"That's quite enough about what I'm *not.*" I was sexy and independent and I could do far worse than to have some traits in common with forthright Amanda or big-hearted Carrie. I could also do far *better* than this creep. I held out my hand and uttered the time-honored restaurant phrase that signaled we were done. "Check, please."

I wasn't certain yet what my next job or who my

next lover would be, but the sooner I got out of this stuffy office and away from the pompous man in it, the sooner I could find out.

9

Don't look at these sample menus as rules, just suggestions to get your creativity going. Like passion, food shouldn't come with rigid regulations. Go with what feels right, and trust your instincts.

I SAUNTERED UP TO THE BAR, aware of a little swivel to my hips that hadn't been there when I'd walked into the restaurant. As I approached, Dylan's eyes met mine in the mirrored paneling behind Lewis. Instead of looking away as I had on previous occasions when Dylan had caught me staring, I deliberately held his gaze, letting the corner of my mouth lift in a suggestive smile.

He choked on whatever rich amber liquor he'd been drinking, and I felt cheerfully vindicated for the night we'd first met, when my own soft drink hadn't gone down the right way.

Lewis grinned in greeting, looking dapper in his tuxedo shirt. "Hey, beautiful. You coming back anytime soon?"

"Afraid not." I didn't add that I wasn't planning to come back at all, but I saw Lewis's slight nod and thought he understood.

"Well, can I get you a drink for the road?"

We'd come here in Dylan's vehicle, which was a lot nicer than mine. One strong drink wouldn't hurt anything, and I was in a daring mood. "Tequila shot, please."

If Lewis was surprised that I'd ordered something other than my customary wine, he didn't show it. He shoved a glass across the shiny black counter, a wedge of lemon breaking the perfect circle of salt on the rim. "A toast to our resident author. Congratulations, and good luck on all your future endeavors—books and otherwise."

Dylan and I toasted, then Lewis excused himself, mumbling about needing something from the storeroom.

"The staff obviously adores you," Dylan said, as the bartender made himself scarce.

"Yeah. I'll miss them."

His eyebrows shot up. "Aren't you coming back after the tour?"

"That was the plan." I lifted myself up onto the swivel-stool next to Dylan's. "But, you know, I think I'm ready to move on."

"You've outgrown what they have to offer." He shot a questioning glance to the other side of the room, where Trevor's office door was closed, making it clear that he wasn't talking about just the job.

"Oooh yeah. You know you made him see red?" Positively Bordeaux, if I knew Trevor. I wondered if he would have decided so quickly he needed me back if he hadn't been under the impression he was losing me to someone else. "He thinks there's something between us."

"And did you confirm that?" he asked.

"No. I wasn't going to lie just to make him feel bad, but it didn't matter. He'd already drawn his own conclusions."

Dylan nodded. "What people see means everything, even more than the truth sometimes."

I lifted my tequila, licking the salt away and tilting my head straight back to let the sharp, fiery liquor burn down my throat. Then I slid the lemon between my lips, sucking gently on the cool citrus. Finished, I set the shot glass down and glanced at my companion. "And what do you see? When you look at me, I mean? Just a client?"

He swallowed. "Not 'just,' no."

I smiled. "Glad to hear it. Are you about done with that?"

His gaze went to the mostly empty glass in his hand, and he nodded absently. "We can go. Is there anything else you needed to do today?"

"Yep. But I'd rather wait until you get me home to do it."

THE RIDE HOME was charged. There wasn't much small talk, just some exchanged heated glances. I may have been the one to make the bold pronouncement, but Dylan had been happy to take it from there. He'd escorted me to his car with a subtly possessive hand at the small of my back, his stride purposeful.

I smiled his way a few times, striving for the same worldly confidence I'd—hopefully—projected at Spicy Seas. But now that we were racing back to my place, my heart was pounding a steady beat of *What are you doing? What are you doing?* I wasn't having second thoughts, just that same high-adrenaline excitement you have when you come to the top of the first hill on a roller coaster you waited in line for hours to ride. I was completely looking forward to this—had deliberately set it in motion—but wanting it didn't prevent a few flutters in my stomach.

I knew that, at the very least, I would rectify this

morning's incompleted kiss. Beyond that... I did a quick mental check and was relieved to recall that I was wearing one of my snazzier bras, pink and satiny. As an added bonus, my panties even matched. Whether or not Dylan would find this out for himself, I didn't know, but it never hurt to be prepared.

Mental note for next book—when talking about dinner date arrangements like using nice dishes and matching silverware, I could also remind women to wear coordinating undergarments and guys to avoid anything going threadbare.

I blinked as Dylan pulled into a parking spot outside my building. In all the times I'd made the drive from my place to the restaurant, I didn't remember it ever being so short. Then my hormones kicked in, demanding, "Get this man inside!"

A sound plan.

I hopped out and met him in front of the car. He took my hand in his, only letting go when I needed to unlock the door.

Inside, Dylan stood in the entryway, hitching one eyebrow in roguish challenge. "Well, now that you have me here... This morning you gave me extremely helpful instructions in the kitchen. Was there something else you wanted to talk me through?"

"No." I moistened my lips. "It might be better if I just showed you."

He nodded sagely, his expression solemn except for the glint in his eyes. "I think you'll find I'm a willing pupil."

Rising up on my toes to make up for the difference in our heights, I slid my hands along his back, feeling his warmth and firm muscles. I brushed my mouth against his, loving that first brief contact, the zing in the pit of my stomach, as the roller coaster went soaring down in an exhilarating blur. He tasted good, like Scotch and man. Smooth, sophisticated, very sexy man.

Some guys kiss with an assertiveness, for lack of a better description, moving further and further into the kiss as if they're trying to back you into a corner. Dylan wasn't backing anyone anywhere. He kissed as though he were trying to lure me into a sensual paradise.

Lead the way.

I didn't say the words, but I may have telegraphed them with my small moan of pleasure, because he was suddenly walking us toward my living room. The couch allowed us lots of freedom to continue this delicious moment and see where it led, without the presumption of my bedroom. We tumbled onto the sofa with the kiss still unbroken, like some sort of perfect movie embrace. It was so magical I half expected a musical score and possibly even happy woodland creatures.

I'd forgotten how amazing it could be just to kiss someone—not as the obligatory farewell on a date or habitual good-night to your lover, but kissing for its own sake. Just savoring the person you were with, the person who was making your body melt like dark chocolate stirred at high heat. I heard something shrill, sounding far away but persistent, and I thought that as far as musical scores went, it would never be a big hit.

Dylan drew back slightly, only to dot my neck with kisses as he asked, "Do you want to answer that?"

Ah, the phone. That explained the semi-familiar noise in the distance. But by the time Dylan had finished his question, his lips had found my ear. I wouldn't have budged from the couch just then to save a five-cheese lasagna with made-from-scratch noodles burning in the oven.

"Let the machine—oooh."

He chuckled, his breath ticking the sensitive spot right beneath my earlobe. "Liked that, did you?"

Hell, yes, but before I could say—or better yet, *do*—anything to express my satisfaction, the answering machine did kick on. I heard my own voice echoing from the little table in the hallway, saying I wasn't here right now. Lord I hoped I didn't sound that bad on TV.

Then mechanical-me was replaced by Amanda. "Hey, I'm making good on my promise to call. And to tell you the truth, I really need to talk."

Not now! Judging by the near tremor in her voice, however, I couldn't ignore the call.

To his credit, Dylan was already moving away from me, straightening his rumpled shirt. "I should go?"

No. I nodded as Amanda, in the background, told me she'd be home for a couple of hours and said goodbye. "She works later tonight, so I'd better try to catch her as soon as possible."

"Are you free tomorrow?" he asked.

The hopefulness in his voice earned him another kiss, though it was much briefer than I would have liked.

"Unfortunately, no. Carrie and Eric are going to an afternoon wedding, and I agreed to babysit. I'm not sure how late it will be when they get back."

"Ah, well. Can't blame a guy for asking." He touched his index finger to the tip of my nose. Thank goodness it was nowhere more erotic, or poor Amanda might have been abandoned to deal with her troubles on her own.

WHEN I RETURNED Amanda's call, we decided to meet for dinner at a place near her bar, giving her a very short trip to work and maximizing our time to chat. It didn't take me long to get ready—my shoes were still on and I just needed to run a brush through my hair—but I paused when I saw the woman in the mirror.

Her cheeks were flushed, her brown eyes warm and bright, and her slightly swollen lips were curved in a pleased smile. The whole picture was framed by tousled golden hair. This was definitely the woman who had written *Six Course Seduction.* A woman who could write about aphrodisiacs with no embarrassment and go after what she wanted...especially when that meant a hot consultant. I felt a little high at the moment, partly from the rush of Dylan's kisses, but also from the thrill of instigating those kisses.

Trying to stifle my euphoria so that I could devote all of my attention to my friend, I floated into the small Italian restaurant, decorated in red and green and sculpted resin grapevines. Overhead, "Amore" played, and the lyrics—which, to be honest, I'd always found a little silly—made me grin. Suddenly, a pizza moon hitting me in the eye just seemed to make sense.

"Wow," Amanda said from where she sat waiting on a wrought-iron bench near the restrooms. "If I didn't know you better, I'd say that was an I-got-laid smile."

"Amanda!" I glanced from the hostess tucking inserts into menus to the three little old ladies emerging from the restroom. "I most certainly did *not.*" Of course, if she'd timed her need to talk a little differently, who knew? But even if I had, I wouldn't waltz into the nearest *ristorante* and announce it to anyone within earshot.

My friend stood, grinning. "Hey, I said *if.*" Wearing a low-cut, pin-striped imitation of a man's business shirt, untucked over tight jeans, she looked more herself than she'd sounded on the phone earlier.

The hostess showed us to one of those space-conserving mini-booths made just for two that I found annoying in their attempts to squeeze more people into the dining room. Restaurants should be about atmosphere as much as seating capacity, and besides, if I'd been a pants size larger, there could have been serious lopping-into-the-aisle issues.

"So?" I prompted when Amanda and I were alone. Neither one of us bothered reaching for our menus. We both knew I was getting the stuffed eggplant, and she was having the meatballs. "You sounded…on edge in your message." Not quite upset, but not herself, either.

"I was startled," she said. "I may be in love."

"*What?*" Okay, this morning was the first I'd heard there was a possible object of affection on her radar screen; now she was in love? I knew a few women who were quickly infatuated and thinking long-term thoughts, but Amanda wasn't one of them. Her relationships veered toward casual, and I couldn't remember the last time I'd heard her tossing around the *L*-word.

"See? You're startled, too."

"No. Stunned. I mean, I think it's a good thing, but when…? Who? How?"

The corner of her mouth quirked, amusement over my reaction momentarily displacing any distress she felt. "At the bar."

"Not Todd?"

Her nose crinkled. "Of course not. It's a patron. Richard, Richard McNally. He's been coming in for a while."

"Then why—" I broke off so that we could rapidly place orders, then returned to my question. "Then why is this the first I'm hearing of him?"

Amanda bit her lip. Where did she find such

smudge-proof lipstick, anyway? I knew she'd look as perfectly made-up when she announced last call hours from now. "He's not…my type."

"Don't take this the wrong way, but I thought your usual type was male. Not that you aren't discerning, but it isn't as if you only go out with blondes or Caucasians or computer programmers."

"Well, for starters he's been married before, and has a daughter."

"Oh." She was just full of surprises today—I'd never seen her involved with someone who had a child. Amanda was usually philosophical about parting ways with a lover, but she was adamant about not wanting those goodbyes to complicate a kid's life.

"And he's a little older."

"Like when you said Todd's crush on you was of the older-woman variety?"

"No. Bit more of an age difference than that. And he can be old-fashioned."

I raised my eyebrows, lowering my gaze from her scarlet not-even-a-nuclear-blast-would-faze-me lipstick to her impressive cleavage revealed by an unfastened top button. "You're right. He doesn't sound like your type."

She shrugged, but her eyes were vulnerable, making me regret my teasing. "He's a history professor, and I think all that research about courtly manners has screwed up his modern perspective or something. Plus, he married his high-school sweetheart. They were together a long time before she died, since they were kids. I mean, he's, um, only ever been… I feel ridiculous trying to say this."

The light dawned. "He's only ever cooked in one kitchen? Sorry, it was the best I could do," I said in response to her groan.

Glancing away, toward a suddenly mesmerizing oil painting of Venice, she was quiet. I almost didn't hear her when she asked, "Kind of makes you wonder what a guy like that would see in me, doesn't it?"

"Hell, no, it doesn't! Off the top of my head, I'd say he might be interested in your sense of humor, your honest nature, your loyalty and protectiveness toward others." It was surreal to see Amanda expressing any kind of self-doubt. Shouldn't that be *me?* She was usually the kick-ass confident one.

Our meals came, and Amanda attacked one meatball with gusto.

I grinned. "What was that business you gave me the other day, about people with infatuations losing their appetites?" She'd been nervously chowing down on something every time I'd seen her lately.

"Misdirection?"

"Did you really not want me to know?" Intellectually, I should be the first person to respect her right not to mention it, but I had to admit I was feeling a little wounded.

"I wasn't sure there was anything worth mentioning. The first time he came in was on his—their—wedding anniversary. He wanted a couple of drinks, and I could tell he was down, so we ended up talking. I thought he was attractive, but I don't generally try to pick up men who are mourning their late wives. Besides, the way he talked about her, I didn't think he even realized I was a woman. That really drew me to him, though, you know? How much he cherished her. I didn't see him for a few weeks, then he came in one night, looking different."

"Different how?" I asked when she got sidetracked by her own fond memories and momentarily forgot my presence.

"Spiffier. A shirt so stiff I don't think he'd ever worn it before. Cologne. A little bit of nervousness in his expression. He had two drinks, left a huge tip and chatted with me on and off for over an hour. We got to be friends."

I smiled. A guy doesn't need new cologne just to make buddies.

Amanda caught my knowing expression—it was fun to be the one giving it for a change. "Yeah, all right. I got to thinking maybe…but that's when he mentioned having a daughter."

"I know you normally avoid that, but give the kid a chance. I'll bet she—"

"That was kind of the problem. She's not exactly a kid. Richard's close to fifty, and Elizabeth is seventeen, going off to an Ivy League college next fall. He didn't know how she'd feel about his getting back into dating, and I could just imagine her reaction. Technically, I'm closer to *her* age than her dad's, and the nearest I ever got to a formal education was Mixers U. I figured she'd assume I was some kind of floozy."

"Amanda, you're terrific, and once she gets to know you—"

When my friend glanced up, her eyes were shining with tears she quickly blinked back. "She's as amazing as he is! I met her today, and when he very obviously went out of his way to give us girls a moment alone, she told me she was grateful for making him smile again."

"That's where you went today?" I thought about the phone call in my kitchen earlier.

"Yeah. He finally got up the nerve to mention me to her as they were on their way for brunch, and she insisted he invite me to come along. I was terrified, but damn, I'm glad I went with them."

"I am so happy for you!"

So happy, in fact, that I listened intently for the next hour and a half as Amanda told me all about Richard, how he came from a wealthy family but had rejected the family business to pursue his love of academics, how Elizabeth had shyly extended the invitation for Amanda to come see her in a school play, and how for the first time since puberty, Amanda was actually nervous about taking the next physical step with someone.

She chatted right up until she needed to leave for work, and by the time I got home, I was contentedly envisioning catering Amanda and Richard's eventual wedding. Since it was obvious how important he was to her, I hadn't wanted to interrupt with the revelation that Dylan and I had been making out when she called. Figured. I finally make it through a whole meal where no one comments on my love life, and for a change, I had someone I wanted to talk about.

10

Remember, it's not just about the cooking—there's a lot to be said for the presentation.

DO-IT-YOURSELF home whitening strips are not all they're cracked up to be. This is the conclusion I came to around eleven o'clock Sunday night, after I'd herded Lyssa and Lana to bed for what felt like the four-hundred-and-sixteenth time.

Both girls had insisted at least twice after being tucked in that they had to use the bathroom, though suspiciously little happened during these visits. Then Lyssa had decided that her Beauty and the Beast sheets were way too scary. Looking at the Beast in the dim illumination of her night-light, I had to concede the kid's point, so we'd completely changed her bed linens. Then Lana had asked for water, but I wasn't born yesterday. More beverages equaled more field trips to the potty.

When I realized it was nearing eleven and neither girl showed the slightest sign of being tired, I had to revisit my long-held assumption that Carrie's sleeping schedule was more "normal" than mine. How did she stay so upbeat all the time when it appeared her daughters might keep her awake until midnight, and I knew full well they were often up again with the sun? Thankfully, however, the girls went from sixty to zero in a surprisingly short span. Cries of "Aunt Miriam, I need..." were replaced by delicate pseudo-snores.

Since Carrie and Eric had said they would probably be late, making the most of their childless night to catch up with friends they rarely saw, I had brought some things to do, including teeth whitening. My first television appearance was Tuesday, so I might as well do whatever I could to make it a positive experience.

Then again, if I succeeded with flying colors, did that mean Dylan would nod proudly, get in his car and disappear from my life? We'd mostly discussed getting me ready and hadn't really talked about when he would be going. Recalling his kisses yesterday, I felt a pang of dread in my stomach at the thought of saying goodbye already.

Wanting something else to focus on, I unwrapped the little cardboard carton that promised "three shades whiter in thirty minutes." I had skipped the kind where you applied the formula to each individual tooth with a tiny brush while trying to keep your lips peeled back and your tongue out of the way, choosing instead gel-like strips that were supposed to "slide easily in place, whitening your teeth while you go about your normal routine." Sounded easy enough.

Except that the top strip wouldn't adhere properly and ended up sliding toward the back of my mouth, lodged between my molars and cheek. As I tried to fix it without gagging, I thought to myself that it was probably best that the commercials didn't mention how these things tasted. The lower strip went on easily enough, but the instructions said you were supposed to keep your mouth open to insure the strips weren't displaced. This turned out to be more difficult—and annoying—than I had thought.

I had just thrown the strips away, thinking that if thirty minutes provided three shades whiter, then I had probably improved by at least one-twentieth, when I heard the door between the kitchen and garage open softly. I met my brother in the hallway, and he said he was going to check in on the girls. Then I found Carrie in the kitchen, pouring herself a glass of milk.

"Hey." She smiled, suppressing a yawn. "You want anything to drink?"

"Um…" The strip instructions had said not to eat or drink anything for an hour afterward. I hated to undo all that progress I'd made with my one-twentieth of a shade. "Nah, I'm good. How was the wedding?"

"Lovely." She put the milk back in the fridge, looking wistful. Carrie is a definite romantic, and I imagine she'd even enjoy total strangers' weddings. "The bride was beautiful, and they were so in love."

I sat at the kitchen table, in one of the chairs that didn't have a pink or lavender booster seat. "Speaking of romance, I—"

Her face crumbled. "You've noticed it, too, haven't you?"

"What?" I had no idea what she was talking about, but it obviously had nothing to do with Dylan and my sudden bizarre need to talk to someone about him.

"Night, ladies." Eric peeked his head around the corner. "The girls are sleeping soundly. Thanks for watching them, sis. See you at that book signing this week?"

I nodded. My first autographing was Friday, the book's official release date, and my mother was throwing me a launch party afterward.

When my brother padded off down the hall, I turned

back to Carrie and was surprised to find her watching after him with eyes that looked suspiciously damp. "You okay?"

"No! That's what I'm talking about. Did he kiss me good-night? Of course not. Did he comment on the way I looked today? No. And it's not like I'm vain or anything." She dropped into a chair, kicking off the dark green pumps that matched her dress. "It's just that when you've spent the last few years wearing applesauce and finger paint as often as you've worn a skirt... Do you know he's actually been talking about maybe—maybe—"

Her voice broke on the second *maybe,* and I shot to my feet, glancing around for a box of tissues. Or cookies. Anything that would comfort her and take her mind off of whatever my brother had done.

"Having another baby," she finished miserably, wiping her eyes with the back of her hand.

"Oh." Somehow, that hadn't been what I'd expected. I sat. "And you don't want any more?"

"I don't know. The girls are a handful, but they're also the joy of my life. I have to admit, I do still sometimes get that twinge, you know the urge to hold a new baby. To smell one."

Granted, my experience was more limited than hers, but the smells *I* associated with newborns weren't ones I'd get nostalgic for. "So, you're upset because you can't decide?"

"It isn't that, exactly. Miriam, am I fat?"

I blinked, wondering if she was upset about more than one thing here, or if they were related somehow. "No. Why would you think that?" She wasn't a twig, but she was generally considered by all who knew her to be an attractive woman.

"The couple you met earlier this week, you should have seen the way they looked at each other! And the newlyweds tonight...sometimes I think when Eric looks at me, all he sees is a mom. The person who drives the minivan, keeps groceries around here and cleans the bathroom. I mean, sure we still have sex, but just the basic stuff. He hardly ever—"

"Erk." I didn't consciously interrupt, but I couldn't stifle the small sound of protest at hearing about my brother's performance in the sack.

Carrie's expression was instantly apologetic. "Oops, forgot who I was talking to for a moment. You don't want to hear about our marriage problems." She went to the sink and rinsed out her glass.

Actually, I did. Well, maybe not in grisly detail, but I wanted to help if possible. And I couldn't just leave when she was upset. "Carrie, have you talked to Eric about this?"

"Of course! We've always had a very open channel of communication. He told me I was crazy, that he thought I was even more beautiful now than I was when we got married. Then he kissed me on the forehead, rolled over and went to sleep."

Not exactly the proof of white-hot lust she'd been looking for, then. It was interesting to learn that for all his soul-baring, my brother was still as insensitive as most normal guys.

She shot me a hopeful glance. "You have any thoughts on putting the va-voom back in my marriage?"

"Considering the reasons Trevor dumped me, I think you're asking the wrong woman."

"Trevor dumped you because Trevor is an idiot," she said. "And I thought maybe there was something in your cookbook I could try. You've known Eric longer than I have, so if you have any suggestions..."

For putting the moves on him? Ewww. I tried to pretend she was Amanda, discussing a guy I'd never met instead of one I'd grown up with. "I'll think about the recipes and get back to you, okay?"

"Sure. Call me sometime, or maybe we could even have lunch." At least she was smiling now. "We should talk like this more. This has been really great, Miriam."

"You betcha."

AS IT TURNED OUT, Carrie wasn't the only one who wanted to get my advice on her love life. The producer of *Good Morning Westbridge,* already not my favorite person because he was so annoyingly cheery at seven in the morning, had introduced me to the makeup artist, Leah Peters, with something of a wink and a nudge. Moments later, short, sprightly Leah was confiding that she had an anniversary coming up and wanted to know what she should serve for dinner. She explained that she and her husband had already shared a number of impressive kitchen exploits, and she wanted to top them.

As she asked my opinion on oysters—number-one aphrodisiac for a reason or too cliché?—she directed me to a side room of sorts, a three-sided shallow cubicle that was dominated by a lighted mirror and opened into what appeared to be a catchall area for everything from waiting guests to storing a still-decorated Christmas tree. Leah dug through an enormous tackle box of makeup, still quizzing me on what she should serve for her night of love, and I settled into a tall padded chair with the promise to autograph her one of the advance copies I had in my car, so she could pick out for herself what looked good. But then somehow we went from her asking for suggestions to her wanting to share salacious tips for me to include in future books.

I squirmed in the chair, now knowing far more than I'd ever wanted to about the use of pudding in her marriage. It was way too early for this level of over-information! The worst part was I couldn't escape—at least not until I was wearing noticeably more makeup than the man who would be interviewing me. I was the hostage of a woman wielding a MAC contour brush.

I grimaced as she launched into another frolicking tale, this one apparently involving salad. She said something about cherry tomatoes, then chided that I shouldn't close my eyes so tightly. I fluttered my eyelids, trying to keep them in optimal position for makeup application, but when I heard the word *cucumber,* I panicked. Enough was enough! If she was so anxious to get all this information out into the public, she could write her own book.

I drew back, aware that I would be lucky not to have mascara streaked across my cheek. "You know—"

"How's everything going over here?"

"Dylan!" I turned toward my rescuer, thrilled by the sound of his voice—the first time I'd heard it since Saturday. I had half expected him to call yesterday, then tried his cell-phone number myself in the evening. I hadn't known what to say to his voice mail beyond a fairly lame "So I guess I'll see you at the studio tomorrow," which had been my attempt at casual.

"Miriam. You look great." The words weren't overtly personal, but his husky undertone sent a thrill through me. Did other people hear it, too? "All ready for your first live interview?"

Even if I hadn't been, the appreciation in his eyes would certainly bolster my confidence. I crossed my legs, aware that he was watching them beneath the flirty black skirt I wore. Whatever he'd been up to since I'd seen him last, he didn't appear to regret our kisses.

"I think so." I batted my lashes at him. "I've had a pretty good coach helping me prepare."

He grinned. "Glad you feel that way, because don't forget you have that cooking segment for WFD to tape this afternoon."

That piece wouldn't be live, just recorded as part of a local cable show aired on the weekend. I loved the thought of anything stupid I said being edited out. Wouldn't it be great if life worked that way?

The makeup artist with the pixie features and shock of red hair cleared her throat delicately, either because it was tough to apply lipstick to someone when her mouth was moving or because I hadn't yet introduced her to the gorgeous hunk of man who had interrupted us.

"Dylan, this is Leah Peters, their wonderful makeup artist." Always a good rule of thumb to be nice to the person responsible for what your face is about to look like. "Leah, Dylan Kincaid, my media consultant."

"Lucky girl," Leah breathed at a volume only I could hear. Then she stepped forward to shake Dylan's hand. "Nice to meet you. You have a fabulous jaw...and cheekbones. Ever do television?"

He shook his head. "No, I don't have any ambitions to be in the spotlight myself. My talent is working with others to develop their potential, helping *them* shoot for stardom."

I almost guffawed. I was more like a firefly than a star, so I hoped he wasn't counting on me to pad his résumé.

"Well, if you don't mind, I'm going to get back to

helping our star shine," Leah said, waiting until Dylan had excused himself to find coffee before asking, "Are you two an item? A guy like that could inspire any girl to write a steamy book."

I just smiled mysteriously, taking Dylan's interview advice to let them wonder once in a while. Plus, I didn't really know where we rated on the "item" scale.

When Leah was finished with me, I met Dylan and the producer over by the side of the studio, which looked far smaller than it did on television. There was a news desk where two anchors reported entertainment tidbits and local interest stories, a blank bright blue screen where a meteorologist was currently pointing at invisible fronts and coastlines I assumed the viewers at home could see, and then two tiny love seats with a fern in the background. That small, homey setting was where Stephen Gerard would interview me in a few minutes. I'd been briefly introduced to the handsome host before Leah whisked me away to work her cosmetic magic.

The producer was firing instructions at me as I approached. "The light man, Henry, also does sound. He'll wire you while Chloe and Jake do the Hollywood Minute, then we'll cut to commercial and come back to you and Stephen. Sound good?"

I nodded and found myself steered toward the love seats. To give myself an idea of what to expect, I had taped a couple of last week's *Good Morning Westbridge* broadcasts (I tended not to be awake when it normally aired). It looked relatively harmless, but I still experienced a flutter of anxiety as Stephen Gerard came to take his seat.

"Hi." The dark-haired man flashed a reassuring smile. "Nervous?"

"Maybe a little," I said from around Henry, a burly man with a mustache…who was sticking his hand inside my shirt?

"Just taping the microphone in place, ma'am," said Henry. "Don't mind me."

Right. *Pay no attention to the man with his hand down your cleavage.* Okay, maybe not quite my cleavage, as the mike ended up low in the collar of my blouse and nowhere obscene. Still, Henry was closer to the goods than I generally allowed men whose last names I didn't know. Good thing I hadn't gone for the really assertive push-up bra.

While Henry was giving me a cheap thrill for the morning, the producer monitoring the video feed asked me to look up for a moment. Stephen only had half my attention as he explained he'd thoroughly enjoyed the copy of *Six Course Seduction* he'd been sent prior to the interview. I started to thank him, but was distracted by the light meter Henry suddenly held in front of my face.

Then Henry was out of the way, the producer was giving us the thumbs-up, and we were apparently coming back from commercial. Yipes! I cast a panicked look at Dylan, who graced me with a slow, sensual smile that made me think about our kiss. I suspected he was deliberately trying to remind me about sex appeal and presenting a flirtatious image, in which case…job well done. I only wished that I were alone with him and not dozens of tuned-in viewers. Then again, for all I knew, nobody watched *Good Morning Westbridge.*

Stephen flashed a bright host's smile at one of the three cameras at the front of the studio. "Good morning. If you're just tuning in, I'm pleased to announce that I have as my guest today the lovely Chef Miriam

Scott, author of *Six Course Seduction,* a witty and provocative cookbook for lovers that will be in stores later this week. Thank you for being with us, Miriam."

My smile felt stiffer than I would have liked, but that could have just been all the makeup Leah had applied. "Thanks for having me. I'm eager to get the word out about *Six Course Seduction,* in case I can help inject a little extra romance into anyone's Valentine's Day out there."

"From everything I read, I'd say you're just the person to do that. I have to admit, I live one of those bachelor lifestyles where the extent of my cooking is either a frozen pizza or charring something on the grill, but after reading your book, I was ready to enroll in a cooking class—especially if all chefs look like you," he added.

Though I suspected his low-key flirting was more for the audience's benefit than mine, his comment was made with enough boyish sincerity that my smile widened. "Charmer. I doubt you need much help winning over women, but if you're looking for tips, dessert is always a nice start. Even someone intimidated by the thought of preparing a whole dinner from the book can handle something as simple as frozen red grapes rolled in sugar and chocolate. Or slice up some apples and melt caramel. The finger-food experience of dipping the apples and feeding them to your lover is sure to help set the mood. It could be a nice surprise, to bring your date back to your place for a little pampering after dinner."

"You mentioned in your book that apples have been considered a 'food of love' in numerous cultures throughout the ages. The same goes for pumpkin seeds, ginger, artichokes and a whole array of foods I never knew were sexy. I understand it's common for chefs to test their recipes." His grin held a note of playful suggestiveness. "Would you say the research for this cookbook was more *involved* than others?"

I folded my hands primly and cast an angelic look upward, rather enjoying myself. "I'm sure you understand that a great chef, like a great magician, can't give away *all* her secrets."

"Can't blame a guy for asking." He chuckled, then gave another plug for my book and its Friday release date as he reminded viewers to come back after commercial for more from me and to get information on a charity golf tournament coming up in a few weeks.

While he addressed the cameras, I recalled Dylan saying those same words to me the other day—*Can't blame a guy for asking.* He'd been seeking more time alone with me. Feeling warm and eager for that time alone, I cast a glance in his direction, but stopped dead at the look I caught on his face.

His expression, which he couldn't quite mask before I glimpsed the almost appalled regret, put me in mind of Dr. Frankenstein second-guessing himself once the monster had been brought to life.

11

Chocolate as an aphrodisiac may have scientific basis, as it contains phenylethylamine—a "pleasure" chemical to our brain. Some have said chocolate can replace sex. I say, if that's the case, you're not having the right sex.

THE SECOND HALF of the interview with Stephen wasn't as much fun as the first, preoccupied as I was with my glowering image consultant, but I still felt that I did a good job. I was glad the experience had been with someone as personable as Stephen and appreciated his efforts to make the book sound so scintillating. As I was removing the microphone, I thanked him for going easy on a rookie.

He grinned, rising from his seat. "If you're interested in picking up tips for the other interviews you're doing, I'd be happy to give you some pointers. Maybe over dinner tonight?"

I blinked. Was he asking me out on a date? I hadn't thought the flirting throughout our segment had been anything more than showmanship.

"It's nice of you to offer," a male voice said from beside me—causing me to jump since I hadn't realized Dylan was standing there. "But Hargrave's already paying me to give Miriam those pointers. You wouldn't want to put me out of a job."

He swung his gaze toward me. "And your afternoon is just packed solid, with that cooking demonstration and everything."

My jaw dropped. What *everything?* There was only the demonstration, and had Dylan just turned down a date on my behalf? I was too bemused by what seemed very much like jealousy on his part to know what to say.

I thanked Stephen again and said goodbye to the producer, carefully fostering good relations in case I did a publicity round for the next book. I didn't say anything to Dylan until we were alone, out in the station's parking lot.

"So, did I live up to your expectations?" I asked him. "Because, frankly, I thought I was doing pretty well. But judging by the look on your face—"

"I'm sorry." He ran a hand through his hair. "That was beyond inappropriate. You have every right to go to dinner with Stephen bloody Gerard, if that's what you want. Although I can't imagine *why* it would be. He's so—I'm sorry."

I laughed. "Do your apologies always come out sounding so ungracious?"

He stopped, more or less pinning me between his body and my car. "Is going out with Gerard what you want?"

"Of course not." The memory of Dylan's mouth on mine shivered through my body, and I willed it to show in my eyes when I looked at him, to conjure the same memory in him. This deliberate flirting was fairly new, but judging by his choppy breathing, it was effective. "I thought I made it clear the other day what I wanted."

I saw a flash of relief in his gaze just before his eyes darkened with desire. "Good." He tipped my chin up with his index finger, but I was already lifting my face toward his.

His lips were more demanding, more possessive than they'd been the last time, and though I would never have admitted it, I was delighted. I couldn't remember any of my past boyfriends being jealous over me, or anyone giving them real reason to be. Obviously no girl wants to be involved with a distrustful lover, but having a hot guy show the occasional flash of insecurity over losing you to someone else wasn't all bad.

My confidence and latent seductress tendencies had been aroused by the morning's events, and I nipped at Dylan's lower lip teasingly before deepening the kiss, sliding my tongue into his mouth, sucking at his. When we finally stopped to come up for air, I sighed.

"I missed you yesterday." The words were out before I could censor myself, but given his reaction to my possibly going out with another man, I figured the sentiment wasn't inappropriate.

"I was drumming up some business," he told me. "There's nothing concrete in Atlanta that needs immediate attention, so I followed up with some contacts in the area. I thought perhaps I could stay a little longer than I'd first intended...."

My body melted despite the chilly breeze and my relatively short skirt. I knew "a little longer" might mean nothing more than a day or two, but the fact that he was in no hurry to rush off was nice.

"I'm glad," I told him. "I like having you around."

His eyes danced with amusement. "I don't make you nervous anymore, then?"

"When did you ever make me nervous?" I retorted with mock indignation.

"Oh, so getting flustered that often is normal for you?"

I shrugged, a sheepish smile forming. "Not all of us are polished and poised."

He dropped his hands to my waist, pulling me closer for the very adult version of a hug—less arms, more full frontal contact. "You were extremely polished today. I'll admit, even though I coached you to be flirtatious, it threw me, watching you bat your eyelashes at a good-looking local personality. But that doesn't change the fact that you had him eating out of your hand. You're a natural!"

"Thank you." The pride and admiration in his tone made me feel good about the publicity events yet to come, but at the same time I couldn't help thinking that his words were unintentionally ironic. Which part of forcing myself out of bed at a foreign hour, being shellacked in makeup and spending twenty minutes focused on projecting an image was *natural?*

NOT THAT I HAD MUCH to base it on in the way of comparison, but I felt that my cooking segment that afternoon went off without a hitch. It was to fill a "how-to" slot in a weekly program, so there was no host, just me doing my thing. I'd spent so many nights cooking alone in my apartment that the hardest part was to remember to give instructions to the absent audience, but looking up and addressing Dylan behind the cameras was good incentive. In my mind, it became a private cooking lesson. He certainly looked hungry by the time I'd finished preparing the empanadas.

After the videotaping, we called Joan to let her know the first two shows had gone well. I thought it might be funny to tell her I'd inadvertently burned down a television studio, but decided against it. Instead, I thanked her profusely for sending Dylan my way. My cheeks warmed as I spoke, but I hoped that my feelings for Dylan weren't obvious on the phone. When he and I went to dinner later, though, we both knew that it was a date, not business. He made mention of the other interviews this week and the book signings he and Hargrave had lined up, but the shared glances and occasional touches were strictly personal. We chatted about everything and nothing, from the people in our lives we liked to the movies we didn't. I wished we could go on talking for hours, but he'd already mentioned meeting with a short-term client in the morning, while my getting up at the crack of dawn was catching up to me.

"There's something I wanted to ask you," I told him as we sipped our after-dinner coffee, though frankly not even caffeine was going to keep me alert and energetic much longer. "You said you would be at the signing Friday—"

"Your first one, I wouldn't miss it."

I smiled at the note of pride in his voice. "Thanks. But I wanted to talk to you about after the autographing. My mom's throwing a party back at my parents' place, and I wondered if you might like to come…as my date."

He grinned, reaching across the table to lay his hand on mine, brushing his thumb over my knuckles. "Not just your 'TV guy'? I'd love to."

I laughed, remembering his introduction to my brother and sister-in-law. "Carrie and Eric will be there, so that's at least two people you know."

"You think the prospect of meeting new people intimidates me?" He seemed amused by this, which, given his job, was understandable.

"Oops. Guess I was confusing you with me. It should be fun, although my family can be...gregarious." I wasn't putting them down—there were worse things than relatives taking an exuberant interest in your life—but I felt he should be warned. Another thought dawned, and I bit my lip. "Eric almost recognized you the other day. He was a big fan of, um, your father's." As absurd as it sounds, I had practically forgotten I was hanging out with the son of a rock star.

"Lots of people were," Dylan said matter-of-factly.

"But he'll probably figure out who you are."

He shrugged. "It's not a secret."

"Just not something you like to talk about?"

"I was here on business. I focus on my clients and their needs, not my background." He moved his hand away from mine, fiddling restlessly with the spoon he'd used to stir creamer into his coffee. "I'm guessing you weren't a fan of J.D.'s music? You're one of the few people who knows who my parents are and doesn't ask much about them. Most of your questions have been about *me*."

He sounded almost awed by that, which would have been funny if it weren't a little sad. If the man didn't realize he was enough to hold a woman's attention all by himself, he just wasn't paying attention.

"I care about you." I'd meant it as a simple statement of fact, but it came out sounding breathy and fraught with emotional implication or something. Possibly over the top, considering I hadn't known him that long. Then again, I'd known Trevor for ages, and where had that gotten me?

Dylan grinned. "I'm glad. But you're a caring person by nature."

"Me?" Huh. I didn't kick puppies or anything, but I'd

always thought of myself as more aloof than touchy-feely.

"Sure. It was obvious just from the few people I met at the restaurant how much your staff likes you, and you and Amanda are clearly there for each other. And I read your book, remember? A woman that sensual, so tapped into emotions and reactions, can't help but be attuned to those around her."

Maybe this was the wrong time to confess I'd mostly bluffed my way through the writing, feeling somewhat like a fraud the entire time.

His expression grew naughty, and he dropped his voice to a low, confiding tone. "To be honest, that was probably the first time I imagined kissing you—while reading *Six Course Seduction* the day after we met. I believe it was the section on strawberries that did me in. By the time I was finished, I felt as if I knew you, and I was wildly intrigued."

"I… Really?"

The waitress brought our check, and I stared at the lacy pattern of the tablecloth, my stomach turning over. He'd felt as if he knew me? Interesting, because when I'd read through the final proofs of my book before it had gone to print, at times the words had seemed like those of a stranger. Or, if not a stranger, maybe Amanda—as though I'd been channeling her attitude and experience in my determination to do something daring and noticeable.

She had told me the book was more me than I realized, and while I was beginning to agree with her a little, I also wondered if Dylan would be equally "intrigued" by the more familiar part of me who wore navy sweats and watched grade-B horror movies with lamentable special effects.

ON WEDNESDAY, I drove upstate for a couple of hours, to do an interview on the other side of Columbia. I went alone, since Dylan's job was pretty well concluded. He'd prepared me well with his coaching and seen me through both of yesterday's appearances. Outside of my first live appearance, he was done. I smiled, thinking about his plans for the day. He was meeting with a woman who ran a small independent hotel and wanted to update its image and figure out the best way to make it stand out among all the other tourist choices. Maybe it was vain to think Dylan's interest in other Charleston business opportunities was because of me, but if his kisses goodbye at my front door last night were anything to go by, the man enjoyed being with me.

A feeling that was entirely mutual.

I was grinning as I walked inside the television studio, which seemed cool and refreshingly dim compared to the bright morning sun. The host for the interview was a woman, and I wondered how that would affect the persona Dylan had encouraged me to project. I certainly wasn't going to flirt with her, not even in the hopes of reaching a niche sales demographic.

But as it turned out, doing the segment with Ashlee was fun. With Dylan very much on my mind, the interview had that sort of wicked confessional just-between-us-girls feel to it, and Ashlee promised her regular viewers a post-Valentine's Day report on how her fiancé, Marc, liked the example menu we planned on-air. We also did a baking segment together, although the professional chef in me winced at Ashlee's long dark hair hanging over her shoulders as we spiced and stirred. There wasn't time for both preparation and cooking—especially when you took into consideration the chilling time—so though we went through the instructions for the individual raspberry-bourbon chocolate tortes, I had a premade batch ready to show off at the end of our taping. The crew had been salivating over them since I arrived.

Everyone raved over the desserts when we were finished and swore to buy multiple copies of the book. I expected the drive home to leave me feeling drained, but I arrived at my apartment feeling energetic and invigorated. For the first time, I was really looking forward to my book's upcoming release. Granted, it could still potentially flop, but so far everything was exceeding my most optimistic expectations...especially the part where the hunky, charming out-of-towner seemed as attracted to me as I was to him.

Last night, I had been surprisingly worn out, probably because of the anxiety I'd experienced leading up to the actual interviews, and had barely brushed my teeth and listened to the six messages on my machine. Returning calls had been out of the question. Now, I kicked off my shoes and got comfy on my bed. I tried to reach Amanda first, to thank her for taping *Good Morning Westbridge* and congratulating me on the appearance. No answer at her place, and the cell phone went straight to voice mail.

Carrie was on her way out the door for a pediatrician's appointment, so that left my mother for girl talk.

I dialed home, and she answered on the first ring.

"Hello?"

"Hi, Mom. It's Miriam. Sorry I didn't get a chance to call you back last night, but thanks for the message."

"Oh, sweetie, we were just so proud of you! You did a wonderful job on television, and all my friends have been calling. I feel famous. You know, I think that Stephen Gerard liked you. And he was a cutie."

I grinned at the hopeful note in her voice. "Yes, he

was. But actually, Mom, I may be seeing someone. Nothing serious or anything, we've only been on one real dinner date, but I asked him to come with me on Friday night, if that's okay."

"Okay? That's terrific! You know you can count on us to make him feel welcome."

I turned my wry laugh into a cough. Their excluding him hadn't been a concern.

"Speaking of Friday," Mom continued, "I was just headed off to get the groceries we'll need, so I can be back by the time your father comes home. But I'll see you in a couple of days!"

If the people in my life wanted me to open up more, they really needed to be more available for conversation. But the truth was, I had mostly been killing time by returning those calls. The person I most wanted to talk to was Dylan. I just hadn't wanted to interrupt his client meeting.

I checked the digital clock on the nightstand next to my bed, wondering if he was finished. Would I be too clingy if I called him now, after he'd spent all day and yesterday evening with me?

Nah. If nothing else, he was still my media consultant, I rationalized, and he'd want to know how today's cooking demonstration went. Besides, if he was in the middle of a business meeting, he'd probably have his ringer off and I wouldn't interrupt a thing.

"Dylan Kincaid speaking."

All thoughts of business—his or mine—went out of my head as soon as I heard that voice. I grinned into the receiver, glad he couldn't see what was probably a very dopey expression. "Hey. It's Miriam. Did I catch you at a bad time?"

"Nope. I was just grabbing a quick drive-through

lunch before making another stop and trying to foist my services on another contact. How did your morning go?"

"Great. The cooking was a piece of cake, if you'll pardon the pun." Cooking. Dylan. Didn't the man deserve something better than fast-food meals on the fly? Of course he did. He deserved something lovingly made just for him, chock full of vitamins, minerals and subtle amorous suggestion. I suddenly had a very good idea of how to put my restless energy to use. "The reason I called is, are you free for dinner?"

I HADN'T BEEN THIS NERVOUS since the high-intensity "real time" final exam in cooking school. But the best chefs know how to perform under pressure, and my dinner tonight was a masterpiece—from the prosciutto-wrapped melon appetizer to the ginger cake. And to top it off, I didn't look half-bad myself.

Though I'd prioritized dinner preparations over makeup and mostly skipped cosmetics, I'd curled my hair into loose waves that looked artfully rumpled and, with any luck, sexy. I was wearing a midriff-baring deep orange sweater with a pair of low-slung slacks I remembered Dylan eyeing appreciatively on me during our shopping excursion.

My apartment, mostly clean, was aromatic and lit with soft-bulb lamps and a few well-placed jar candles. I figured the dim, romantic lighting would hide any accumulated dust on bookshelves or smudged windows. My kitchen, I keep spotless—the rest of the apartment is often left to fend for itself. I hoped that Dylan, a bachelor who probably wasn't even home often, could relate.

He arrived right on time, grinning his pleasure to see

me and holding out a bottle of pinot noir. "I had no idea what to bring."

"Just yourself would have been all right," I assured him. "But thank you. This is very thoughtful."

He'd joked as he walked me to my car after shopping that his father hadn't taught him to be a gentleman. Well, someone had. I doubted his good manners and warm nature with people were just his projecting a likable image.

While Dylan uncorked the wine, I told him dinner was almost ready. "But I have appetizers if you're already hungry."

"Why am I not surprised?" He leaned against the counter. "If I were cooking for someone, I'd probably dump a bag of Doritos in a bowl and call it hors d'oeuvres. But just so she'd know she was special, I'd make sure to get the ones with *extra* cheesy flavor."

Having witnessed his inexperience in the kitchen, I believed him.

I laughed as I pulled the pork roast out of the oven. "For someone who knows so much about creating the right appearance, you can definitely be a real guy sometimes."

"Thank you. It can be tough to overcome some of the stodgier lessons learned at an old-fashioned British boys' school, but I do try." He looked around. "I'm sure you have everything under control, but is there anything I can do to help?"

"You want to grate cheese over the pasta salad?"

"I'd be happy to."

I reached across him to open the drawer where the grater was, and he caught my wrist, reeling me in toward him.

"Did I mention you look terrific?" he asked.

"So do you." If someone had suddenly clapped their

hands over my eyes and given me a quick pop quiz on what Dylan was wearing, I probably couldn't even have answered. Pants? A dark shirt? I wasn't someone who cared about clothes. But he *did* look terrific—his mouth quirking at the corner in a half smile whenever he glanced at me, his eyes the greenest I'd ever seen them. I was reaching up to kiss him before I even realized my own intentions.

His mouth met mine, and for a change, I genuinely didn't give a damn whether or not the food got cold. It was a good kiss. The kind that you feel all the way down to your toes and makes your stomach somersault in a completely pleasurable way. So I couldn't help a little squeak of muted protest when Dylan abruptly pulled away.

"Wait." He reached for the bottle and poured the wine into one of the glasses I'd set out. Then he held the glass to my lips.

Resisting the urge to point out that he hardly needed alcohol to get somewhere with me, I drank, no sooner lowering the glass than Dylan was kissing me again. Sipping at my lips and sliding his tongue into my mouth as if I were the fine wine to be savored. The action was one I'd recommended in my book, but I'd merely been guessing as to its effectiveness.

I felt my pulse quicken, seeming to echo and throb throughout my body, and chuckled a bit breathlessly when he broke off the kiss. "Handy tip, those wine-flavored kisses. What did you do, take notes while you read?"

"No need. I have an excellent memory." He glanced toward the pasta. "For instance, would that be pine nuts and sun-dried tomatoes?"

I blushed in answer. I hadn't lifted an entire menu straight from *Six Course Seduction,* as that had seemed vaguely crass, commercializing our dinner instead of personalizing it. Also, I figured it would be better if not every single thing I set on the table screamed, "Do me." But the pasta salad had been in the book.

"You know what they say about pine nuts," Dylan drawled, his voice laced with wicked humor. "You aren't by any chance scheming to have your way with me, are you?"

I inhaled deeply, summoning the alter ego that had done a tequila shot and asked to be taken home. "Absolutely. Any problem with that?"

"Not a one."

"Good." I grinned. "I'd hate to ply you with chocolate until you changed your mind, but if that's what it takes…"

He was laughing as he poured his own glass of wine, and moments later, we'd carried the food out to the table. Between flirting with Dylan and talking about our respective days, I managed to get in a few bites of food, but as flooded with anticipation and adrenaline as I was, I could barely taste a thing. I had to take his word for it when he told me dinner was delicious.

"They're going to miss you at Spicy Seas," Dylan said as he enthusiastically finished off his meal. "Do you know where you want to go next?" This is what I loved about Dylan—how he always seemed genuinely interested. He really was a people person.

"I'm still thinking about it," I admitted. "At the time I met Trevor, I was still working my way up, not sure where I wanted to eventually be. Then I got caught up in helping him develop his idea, although if it had been me, I probably wouldn't have opened yet another seafood restaurant.… I don't read many of those women's magazines that Amanda gets, but I know they recommend that you don't spend your date talking about an ex. You have anyone in your past you can chat about so I don't feel so conspicuous?"

Dylan laughed. "Sorry, no. There were women in my past, but no one I almost married. Guess it would help if I was in one place for more than a few months, but nothing's ever really felt like home. Besides, it would be damn near impossible to be thinking about another woman right now."

His eyes met mine, and I swallowed. I hadn't been with a man in a long time, and I very much wanted this one.

I stood, whisking dishes off the table. "Dessert?"

He helped me carry plates and serving bowls to the sink. "What's on the menu?"

"Ginger cake with a cream-cheese icing."

Tilting his head, he took my hands in his and considered. "Cake might be overkill after that dinner...but do you have any leftover icing?"

My throat went dry, my mind suddenly a whir of enticing visuals. "I think you took that book too literally." It had been written with the worldly air of someone who knew her way around a bedroom. While I wasn't exactly without prior experience, I suddenly worried that I might not live up to his expectations.

Dylan ran a finger over my lips, tracing them delicately. "Not at all. But in case there were any fantasies in there that you—"

"Right now, the only fantasy I have is you," I told him, pulling him closer. I was so hungry for him I verged on needy, and I didn't dare give myself time to let the performance anxiety simmer to full boil.

Dylan certainly didn't argue as we kissed our way into my living room. These were not the kisses of before dinner, the kind meant to tantalize and whet the appetite. This was the culmination of being together for the last hour or so, all of our glances or fleeting physical encounters charged with knowing how the evening would end.

He tugged at my sweater, and I held my breath as he lifted it over my head. The bra was a new one, but it did defiantly little to enhance what was already there. What you see is what you get. Thankfully, he seemed pretty happy with what he saw, his gaze avid as he ran his fingers down the side of my breast, the sensation causing my nipples to tighten into hard points.

Though he might joke about a stodgy sentence in an all-boys' school, he'd definitely acquired a well-rounded education about women somewhere along the line. My bra practically melted away under his deft hands. I wasn't quite as suave about getting his shirt off, but since the end result was Dylan's naked chest pressed against mine, I didn't care.

He cupped my breasts, those skilled fingers doing delicious things as we kissed. Our bodies instinctively tried to grind closer, but that would have been easier if we hadn't been standing. And if we hadn't been wearing clothes.

We managed to take care of both of those problems, and I experienced one of those absurd, out-of-body moments where I thought, *Whoa, there's a really hot, naked guy sitting on my couch!* A month ago I would have scoffed at the possibility—or assumed Amanda had sent a stripper into my apartment to make my life more exciting.

Now, however, it seemed right—possibly because I was equally naked as I slid onto his lap, straddling his thighs. The only things between us were a condom and the rest of the night, which might or might not involve a number of dessert toppings from my refrigerator. I moved slowly as I took him inside me, wondering if there would be a twinge of discomfort. It had been a while, after all, and, um, Mother Nature, or whoever was responsible for handing out endowments, had been kind to Dylan.

But there was no discomfort, only a sublime, full-body *mmm,* like the moment you ease your body into a hot, perfect bubble bath, or slide that first piece of dark chocolate between your lips. The moment of blissful contentment was a mirage, however, shattered by the need for more as we moved against each other, kissing and touching and murmuring broken phrases and half-formed words.

One of the smaller candles in the room flickered out, time closing in around us in a meaningless spiral as I arched up and down in Dylan's arms. I could tell by his fervor that he was getting close, but I hadn't realized how close I was until he slipped a hand down between our bodies to where we were joined. His touch was coaxing, firm, teasing me into an orgasm I was still shuddering from when he found his own. The room was suddenly much quieter, and I leaned my head on his sweat-slicked chest, blinking to clear vision that had gone spotty. Eventually, my pulse might even slow down again—it seemed funny to me that it could be racing when my muscles felt so satisfied and relaxed.

Dylan Kincaid was a one-man argument against the old "chocolate is better than sex" adage.

12

Bringing your lover freshly squeezed orange juice in a crystal glass makes a statement. But then, so does handing them a styrofoam cup of coffee along with their clothes and car keys.

I'M SURE THAT IN MY COOKBOOK, I offer some cheeky advice for how to serve breakfast in bed, but the fact of the matter is, in real life, I'm nowhere near as flippant about morning-afters. I'm not my best on *any* day before 10:00 a.m., much less a morning when my alarm clock is shrilling for me to get up while Dylan's curled up alongside me. An innate seductress would probably hit Snooze and kiss her lover awake with some of the same passion we'd generated the night before—*so* not gonna happen.

For one thing, I couldn't reach Snooze. My wrestling with the alarm clock had sent it over the edge of the nightstand and into the blue wicker trash can. Also, how in the name of all that's sacred could I consider kissing anyone when my current breath could be classified as a chemical weapon? Luckily, Dylan was no more of a morning person than I was and, except for some annoyed mumbling at the now-silenced blare of the alarm, showed no signs of life.

I could escape before subjecting him to my breath—

and before he noticed that the artfully rumpled curls of last night had not withstood several passionate encounters and a few hours of sleep. My hair hung around my face in a tangle that would have made Medusa's snakes look sleek and well-coiffed. Motivated by the desire to get out of bed before Dylan discovered how truly scary I was in the morning, I made an impressive transition from yawning and uncoordinated to hot-footing it into the restroom.

Once I had the door shut behind me, I grabbed my toothbrush and tried to figure out what to do now.

Last night had been…wow. Anything I'd ever said about a great meal applied tenfold to making love with Dylan. Delicious. Satisfying. Orgasmic. Kept you coming back for seconds long after your body was saying, "That's probably enough for now." I was a little sore this morning, but I didn't regret any of the three times we'd made love before sunrise.

After the first time, we'd finally gotten around to eating that ginger cake, snacking in the living room while I tried to convince Dylan that an action movie from the sixties was worth watching. He mockingly pointed out that the sound of the punches connecting happened before the hero even swung, and I told him that was all part of the experience. Unconvinced, he'd entertained himself by nibbling on the side of my neck, which had eventually led us to my bedroom.

It had been a very, very long time since I'd had a man in my bedroom. Trevor owned a house, the place I had assumed we'd both live one day, so I'd spent more time there than he had here. Since our breakup, none of my dates had made it that far. Biting my lip, I wondered if Dylan realized that last night had been the exception, rather than the rule. I didn't take sex lightly, but it was possible that writing a book subtitled *From Hors D'Oeuvres to Orgasm* could give a guy the wrong impression.

The shower was blissfully warm, and it was tempting to linger under the spray, but I'd agreed to be the guest "celebrity" instructor at a restaurant downtown that held cooking classes in the morning, before the place opened for lunch. It was another opportunity for me to push the book locally. Next week, I branched out even farther, with a signing at a food festival in North Carolina followed two days later by a television appearance in Atlanta. I hadn't given that specific road trip much thought before now, in terms of Dylan and me, because I figured we would have gone our respective ways by then. But maybe he wouldn't mind letting me crash at his place.

Thoughts along those lines were even more tempting than the shower, and I was creating nifty little fantasies as I toweled off my body, belatedly realizing that I hadn't brought any clothes into the bathroom with me. Logically, I was fully aware that being shy about Dylan seeing me in a just a towel was ridiculous. He'd seen me in a lot less, but still…

I shouldn't have worried about it, though, since he wasn't in my room to catch the peep show. I pulled on a pair of black slacks I'd bought pre-Dylan and a crisp royal-blue blouse, dressing quickly and misbuttoning the blouse twice before I headed toward the front of my apartment.

"Dylan?"

"In the kitchen," he called back. "I made us breakfast."

My heart swelled. The man really was consideration personified. Breakfast was a halved grapefruit and a bowl of whole-grain cereal. But when it's presented by a barefoot, bare-chested blond hunk, I'd take the simple breakfast over mimosas and Belgian waffles any day.

"Did you sleep all right?" I asked him.

He nodded. "Are you kidding? Not to put my endurance in question, but you wore me out."

My cheeks warmed, and I grinned at him. "Ditto. Just, sometimes I have trouble sleeping in a bed that's not mine."

"I've never had that problem. I do fine waking up in strange places. Which is nice, since I travel a lot." He stood, pulling on his shirt from last night. "I've got to get back to my hotel and change, so I'll just shower there."

"Okay, sure." I wished he didn't have to run off, but the fact of the matter was, I'd be late if I didn't head out, too.

I walked him to the door and kissed him goodbye on my tiny porch. He tasted like breath mints, making me feel less guilty that I didn't have a spare toothbrush to offer him. I made a note to ask Amanda whether or not most single women kept those on hand. My medicine cabinet *had* been stocked with condoms, but only because I'd bought some yesterday afternoon.

When we broke off our kiss, I noticed Mrs. Asher next door, retrieving her morning paper and appraising us with arched eyebrows. I stifled a giggle at the thought of my having an indecent reputation. The man sneaking out of my house first thing in the morning sort of went with that whole bright-red, naked-girl book cover.

"Are you free tonight?" Dylan asked.

"Not exactly...Amanda and I had planned to play racquetball this evening and maybe grab dinner." I didn't want to be that woman who canceled on her friends because a cute guy crooked his little finger, but I didn't know how much longer Dylan and I had together before he headed back to Atlanta. I was pretty sure she'd understand, but—

"That's all right. I actually have some calls to make, and I'll see you tomorrow for the signing." He hesitated. "The hotel has my checkout listed as Sunday morning. I was going to drive back to Atlanta and give myself the afternoon before the workweek starts."

"Sunday, huh?" It wasn't exactly breaking news—I'd known he couldn't hang around here giving me fashion tips forever—but I still felt suddenly shaky. "If you wanted, you could, um, check out sooner. Maybe stay here Saturday night? Or even Friday. N-not that I *expect* you to, but the offer's open."

"Are you sure?" He studied my face.

"Yeah." I forced a smile. "You got me spoiled with that whole making-me-breakfast thing."

He laughed. "Wowed you with my skills, did I? And I didn't even have to resort to the impressive frozen waffles."

His teasing prompted a chuckle. "That's because there will never be frozen waffles in my kitchen."

After he'd given me a final kiss and stepped off the curb toward his car, he grinned back in my direction. "Never say never."

AMANDA AND I PLAYED what was possibly the most pitiful racquetball match ever to shame a court. I highly regretted that we'd taken a court with clear walls, instead of one at the end of the hall, enclosed except for the tiny, porthole-styled window in the door. We were both distracted—no doubt by the new men in our lives, a disgrace to feminists everywhere.

"I know we have the court reserved for another fifteen minutes," Amanda said, "but how about we just leave early and go stuff our faces?"

"Deal." Once again proving that people rarely have to twist my arm where food is involved.

Rather than wait at a restaurant, we grabbed a couple of bags of groceries and went back to my place for a really great steak and blue-cheese salad, followed by brownies.

As I mixed the brownie batter, Amanda rinsed out our salad bowls and gave a lengthy description of how things were progressing with Richard. She had definitely decided she was in love with him, yet they were in no hurry to take things to the bedroom. His reticence stemmed partially from having a teenage daughter under the roof, while Amanda wanted this relationship to be markedly different from the ones before it.

"No falling into bed after one or two dates this time," she said vehemently.

My cheeks felt warm. "So, would this be a bad time to admit that Dylan and I fell into bed last night?"

I'd admitted to her even before our woeful racquetball playing that I was attracted to him, which she'd shrugged off as already knowing, and that he was attracted to me.

She goggled at me, her mouth hanging open and her violet eyes full of disbelief. "How could you not have mentioned this earlier?"

I was glad to have it in the open now because I really wanted to talk to her about Dylan, but the couple of times I'd been working myself up to tell her, conversation had moved on too quickly. "We were talking about a whole bunch of other things, and I wasn't sure how to blurt out, 'Oh, and I had sex last night.'"

"It's easy! You say, 'Amanda, great news, I finally had sex again.'"

"Ah. So now I know." I opened the door to the preheated oven and shoved the pan inside.

"How did it happen? Was it here? Was he good? I'll bet he was great. Are you seeing each other again?"

"It was good," I mumbled, feeling my face heat.

She laughed. "I can see we're going to have to ease you into the gossipy girl talk about your relationships."

What constituted a relationship? I knew Dylan cared about me, but did he see a future for us? The way he talked about his life, it sounded as if he enjoyed moving on to new things. But maybe that was just me being insecure.

"He's coming with me to my parents' party tomorrow—"

"You know how sorry I am that I have to work, right?"

I immediately absolved her of the guilt in her expression. "You'll be at the signing. That's plenty of support. And I'll be busy trying to run interference between Dylan and my family, anyway."

She laughed. "Oh, come on, they'll love him."

"Yes, but they can be a lot to take, especially once they find out he's J. D. Kincaid's son."

For the second time that night, Amanda was speechless. Then she began to make little gasping noises, flapping her hands in incomprehensible gestures. She reminded me of a trout flopping on a pier. Short of tossing her into a body of water, I figured the best thing to do was wait until she'd processed this information.

"J. D. Kincaid? *The* J. D. Kincaid? And you've known about this how long?" She narrowed her eyes and placed her hands on her hips. "Anything else you want to tell me?"

"Nope. That about covers it." Except for the fact that I was falling for a funny, considerate guy who had been part of my life less than a month, and that I wasn't sure how that worked with someone who preferred "casual" relationships and was used to "waking up in strange places."

SHORTLY AFTER I'd signed the contract with Hargrave, I'd met another local author, a woman who compiled southern ghost stories. When she'd heard that I'd just sold my first book, she'd shared with me a few of her war stories—including that bane of an author's existence, the book signing. She'd reminisced about the time that the only person who'd stopped to talk to her was someone who'd wanted directions to the Mount Pleasant Towne Center and the time that a little old lady had stalked up to her to complain that the biography section of the store was a disaster, with a slew of books misshelved, insisting that the author fix the problem and not seeming to care that she wasn't actually a store employee.

Apparently the secret weapon that other author had needed was my mother.

When I reached the bookstore, fifteen minutes before the event was scheduled to begin Friday evening, there was already a line. I recognized the women in it as being members of Mom's bridge club. I also spotted people from my parents' church. I had a surreal mental image of inscribing, "Enjoy some of these hot dishes with your hottie," to Pauletta the organist.

But at least the signing wasn't dead. The store manager was downright gleeful when she met me at the table that had been set up.

"I've already asked one of our other locations to send over their copies in case you sell out of these," the brunette informed me, beaming at me from over the rims of her tiny glasses. "And a newspaper called earlier to ask if they could send someone over. It's just a local one, not the city paper, but still..."

I thanked her for coordinating the event and then took a seat at the wooden chair that reminded me of old-fashioned schoolrooms, smiling at people over the stack of bright red hardcover books. I had the sudden premonition that my cheeks were seriously going to hurt in a couple of hours.

My mother swooped out of the women's fiction section to hug me. "My baby! I didn't see you sneak in—I am so proud of you. Now everyone will get to try your fabulous recipes. Who would have thought the little girl who once informed me that people kissing with their mouths open was beyond gross would grow up to write *this?*"

I might have worried that this display was woefully unprofessional if the small crowd assembled hadn't been made up of my mom's friends, and therefore used to displays exactly like this one. Except—oh, hell—as I scanned the line again, I noticed the man who had just slipped through the front door in time to catch my mom's words of praise.

Why couldn't the manager have shoved me discreetly in the back, near the cookbooks? Nope, I was right here front and center. People would practically trip over me getting to the cash register.

Dylan lifted his hand in a little wave, and my heart fluttered at the sight of him. I had definitely rethought my stance on kissing since adolescence.

Twenty minutes later, my hand was cramping and I

had barely had a chance to speak to Dylan, much less introduce him to my mother. Not that I was in a real hurry to do that. While I was trapped here, she'd have him cornered over by sci-fi/fantasy, retelling *Miriam: The Early Years.* And that's if I was *lucky.* There was every chance they'd talk about the book, and what Dylan and I did with frosting was our damn business.

My mother's friends were all very supportive, though a few seemed wounded that I couldn't remember their names, though they'd known me since I was "in diapers." I resisted pointing out that I hadn't seen one or two of them since then and how many of *them* could remember names and events from before their second birthday? Mostly, I just wanted people to stop saying "diapers," and cut me a little slack for confusing Lila Beth Morrow with Lily Belle Martin. When I shoved another copy of the book across the table and glanced to the next customer, I was surprised to find not one of my mother's quilting circle, but a lanky man in his thirties, wearing a windbreaker and a leer.

"So you're the gal who wrote the sexy cookbook, huh?"

"Um…yes. Would you like me to make one out to you?"

He chortled. "The making-out part sounds okay, but I don't think I need a bunch of fancy foods to improve my performance, if you know what I mean."

Gee, no, I was confused by your oblique sexual references, Sparky. And that was the *kindest* retort that sprang to mind. But since I doubted the manager wanted me to antagonize her customers, I suggested, "Then perhaps you know someone who would like it as a gift? Valentine's Day is coming up."

"Nah, I haven't let myself get tied down, so I don't owe anyone a gift."

Casanova was single? Shocker. "Well, thanks for stopping by and saying hi."

He looked as though he would say considerably more, so I craned my neck, looking past him to the next person. But she was talking to the lady behind her and missed my expression of desperation. Luckily, someone else noticed.

Dylan appeared at my side, his hand on my shoulder in an innocent but nonetheless possessive gesture. "You're selling a ton of books, love. Is there anything I can do for you—glass of water?"

Don't you dare leave, I telegraphed with my eyes, although I doubted he would abandon me until the guy who didn't want a book moved on. And I was right. The man glared but wandered off while Dylan and I talked about the reporter who was coming to the signing.

Once the coast was clear, I leaned back a little, letting my head rest against Dylan's waist. "My hero, thanks."

He grinned. "Does this rate higher or lower on the chivalry scale than making your breakfast while you shower? Glad to save you from your own popularity—it's the price of being a sizzling sex symbol, you know."

I was still laughing at that when he left to get me a drink. Now that I wasn't being stalked, water sounded great. I signed a few more copies for Mom's friends and was surprised to notice that a string of strangers had also lined up. Of course, it's possible they thought this was just the line to pay for their purchases and were too embarrassed to say otherwise once they got to the front.

A woman with shoulder-length, wildly curly hair clutched her signed copy to her Clemson Tigers shirt. "I saw you on *Around the House with Ashlee.* You were wonderful. I copied down that torte recipe and plan to build an entire dinner menu with the tips in the book." She leaned forward, lowering her voice to a whisper. "After this weekend, maybe Justin will go ahead and pop the question."

"Oh. Well, good luck to the both of you." I wasn't sure if chocolate would be enough to get her engaged, but it couldn't hurt, right?

I signed another few copies before I noticed that Amanda had arrived—on the arm of a distinguished-looking man who couldn't seem to tear his adoring gaze from her. Richard. I liked him immediately. He was only a few inches taller than my friend, with a handsome face that was aged not so much with lines as character. He was obviously a man who'd seen a lot of both good and bad, but he was still very attractive, the silver streaks at his temples rather flattering with his blue eyes and sandy hair. He looked as if he could have been Robert Redford's long-lost, much younger, equally alliterative brother.

Amanda introduced us and I stood up to shake Richard's hand.

"I'm so glad you guys could make it," I told them.

My friend had never looked so happy. "Richard's heard so much about you, he couldn't resist meeting you. And I've been thinking about a home-cooked meal at my place sometime soon...." She trailed her hand over one of my books.

I managed not to laugh as I autographed a copy. Since I knew Amanda could barely cook toast, I assumed the home-cooked meal was a euphemism. Nonetheless, it was decent of her to buy a book she'd probably never use for anything other than a conversation piece—she could claim credit for being there when I'd brainstormed it, egging me on until there was a hastily scrawled outline.

I grinned at her as she and Richard turned to go after a few minutes of chatting. "I blame you, you know."

She winked. "I know."

The manager had carried two more stacks of books to the table before the line finally wound down to nothing more than an occasional curious passerby who stopped to ask me a question and thumb through the pages. I thanked them all for their time and wished them a nice day.

My mother, however, had missed her calling as a pushy salesperson. "You aren't going to buy a copy?" she asked a young woman with her dark hair in a long braid down her back.

The lady blushed. "I don't, um, have someone special in my life to make any of these things for."

"Perfect!" Mom clapped her hands together, the sound causing the other woman to jump slightly. "Life isn't just about waiting for opportunities, it's about creating them, being ready for them. The right guy is going to come along when you least expect it, and you will have, at your fingertips, the most perfect apple-pie recipe in existence—I know because what my daughter's really done is improve my recipe—and the man's heart will be yours."

She shepherded the woman and a copy of the book toward the cash register before I even had a chance to sign it, chatting the entire way.

I glanced over my shoulder to where Dylan sat on a wooden stool the manager had brought out. "My mother is a nut."

He grinned. "Hey, whatever sells the books. Besides, she does know her apple pie."

A few moments later, a man in a leather jacket, carrying both a notepad and a dictaphone, introduced himself as Jack Carpenter, from the *Dorchester Daily*. He even had a photographer with him who snapped a couple of pictures, one of me signing a book—for my mother since we were temporarily without a real customer—and one of me standing with the store manager in front of the children's section at the front of the store, which seemed ironic, considering my marketing slant.

The interview was pretty simple after the two I'd already had on television. Jack's questions were similar in nature, with one big difference. "And you're the head chef at Spicy Seas?"

I hesitated, figuring the *Dorchester Daily* was not the place to announce my resignation. "That's right."

"Then people can come to the restaurant to get these recipes from the master herself?"

Was it petty if I didn't want Trevor drumming up extra business off my book that he'd so condescendingly pooh-poohed? I gave Jack a saucy smile. "It's a great restaurant, but I think these recipes lend themselves more to intimate dinners in the privacy of your own home."

He chuckled. "Noted. Until recently, you were engaged to the owner Trevor Baines, weren't you?"

I could hardly deny that, not when it had been mentioned repeatedly in the restaurant's original publicity. "Well, I wouldn't say *recently*, but—"

"So is there truth to his claim that he was the inspiration for your book?"

13

> In case of emergency: the escape plan. Sometimes, despite your best efforts and most hopeful intentions, a recipe just doesn't work out. Admit when it's time to call it quits and order a pizza.

"FOR SOMEONE who's the guest of honor, you don't look like you're in a party mood," my date observed.

What tipped him off—the facial tic or clenched fists? Okay, that's an exaggeration, but my expression probably wasn't one of joy.

I was in my parents' crowded living room, sitting on one of the cushions on the hearth of their never-used fireplace, staring into an empty punch cup. "You'd be tired of smiling after that signing, too," I tried to joke.

"You're still upset about that interview?" Dylan asked, standing with his arm against the mantel.

He might not have known me long, but he wasn't an idiot, either.

"Trevor laughed at the idea of the book, and now he wants credit for it?"

"Have to admit, though, the guy's no slouch when it comes to grabbing publicity. That was slick."

I glared up at him. "Could you try not to sound so admiring?"

"Sorry. Didn't mean to. You know I'm on your side."

Right, which was why he'd tried to "help." When Jack's question had left me dumbfounded, Dylan had interjected that *Six Course Seduction* had come about *after* my split with Trevor, once I was romantically and creatively free. He'd hinted without ever saying directly that perhaps the whole reason Trevor and I had broken up was that Trevor hadn't been hot enough for me. I might have appreciated the irony more if it hadn't felt as if we'd just told a newspaper reporter that I was a nympho who had dumped her fiancé and business partner so she could write her racy book.

I sighed, knowing that I was just tired and cranky. Who cared what people thought about my relationship with Trevor? He played no part in my life anymore, and maybe what was really bugging me was how quick Dylan was to make me out to be some kind of sex symbol or how he'd encouraged me to flirt with a couple of guys who'd come into the store after the interview to remind me of the image I'd been projecting to market the book. Apparently, whatever spark of jealousy Stephen Gerard had inspired the other day, Dylan had effectively dealt with it.

"Whatever sells books," I muttered.

Dylan crouched down. "You sold a great many books. You did wonderfully, but it's bigger than just this one cookbook. Do you realize you could become a real personality? Like Martha Stewart—um, pre-scandal, naturally."

People who had thought my writing a steamy cooking manual was a stretch should meet Dylan. His wild ambitions for me were far beyond anything nutty I'd ever dreamed up. "My decorating skills are abysmal. I couldn't even coordinate my clothes without your help, remember?"

He grinned, and I knew he was recalling that day shopping with a lot more lust than he'd allowed himself to show at the time. "Maybe I picked a bad example. There are cooking celebrities who don't make their own homemade wreaths for each season. Emeril!"

Hard to argue with a delusional. "Assuming national syndication can wait for a few hours, I think what I really want is just more of Mom's famous party punch."

Dylan took my cup. "I live to serve."

I smiled at the sexy man with the teasing note in his voice and unfailing support of me, feeling my mood lift a notch. "I'm going to remember that when we get back to my place."

The second Dylan left my side, Eric appeared, as though my brother had been waiting for a chance to talk to me alone.

I heaved a sigh. "Do you want me to ask for his father's autograph or something?" We'd told my family who Dylan's parents were when we first got to the house, before most of the other guests arrived. Eric had been refreshingly nonchalant about it—almost subdued—but now I wondered if he'd just been biding his time.

He scowled at me. "What I want is for you to do something about my wife. She's going nuts with that damn book of yours."

I raised my eyebrows, surprised by his grouchy tone and his apparent belief that I deserved the grouchiness. "What do you mean?"

"You gave us all a copy at that family dinner, and she must have a bee in her bonnet about trying every recipe or something. And it's not just the book. She's been looking up other dishes on the Internet."

"And…you're mad at me because your wife is going through the time and trouble of fixing dinners for you?"

"It's not that." Eric ran a hand over his face. "Maybe a chef wouldn't understand, but sometimes, a guy just wants a burger. Special occasions are one thing, but who wants to come home to green-curry sea bass and goat-cheese starters every night? Mussels with leeks and celery-root puree? I think I hurt her feelings the other night and I didn't mean to, but I don't care what medieval culture considered endives a love charm, I still don't like them."

Hm, possible chapter for the next book: romantic cooking for your finicky sweetheart.

"And it's not just dinners," he continued. "She showed up at the school the other day asking if we could have an on-campus picnic lunch."

Since I was feeling somewhat annoyed with the male species tonight, I felt compelled to defend my sister-in-law. "That sounds very thoughtful."

"It was. We ate portobello sandwiches and had basmati rice, but when we were done, she just kept looking at me with this expectant expression, even though I'd already thanked her several times and told her it tasted great. I mean, what more does she want?"

Yeesh, this is what you get for writing a book that suggests you might know a little something about love—people dumping their romantic problems on you to fix. I patiently pointed out the obvious to my idiot older brother. "Let's see, what do my book and the recipes she's downloading have in common, Eric? Could it be their rumored aphrodisiac ingredients? And if that's the case, what do you *think* she wants, you dolt?"

He blinked, drawing back slightly. I don't think it was my conclusion that surprised him so much as my tone, though. "We were in the school courtyard surrounded by a bunch of adolescents with sack lunches. It's not like I was going to set a sterling non-PDA example by macking on her there."

Dylan cleared his throat, drawing our notice as he held out a cold glass of Mom's sweet bourbon punch.

I was relieved that my brother refrained from discussing problems with his wife in front of a near-stranger. Instead, Eric asked Dylan simple, friendly questions about how he was liking his stay in Charleston.

With a grin in my direction, Dylan answered, "The city's quite hospitable, I've rarely felt so welcome in an unfamiliar place. Miriam showed me around a bit the other day, between her morning and afternoon appearances, and it's great here."

It had been a wonderful few hours, between Dylan's jealous outburst over Stephen Gerard and my cooking segment for cable. I'd taken him by some of the historical buildings and then for lunch to a restaurant tourists had yet to discover. Charleston also had some beautiful gardens, but they were more of a spring attraction. Also, I wasn't sure how much time a guy wanted to spend gawking at flowers. Still, remembering our brief time sightseeing—all the times Dylan had unexpectedly reached for my hand or dropped his own hand to the small of my back as we walked—gave me a warm glow.

That promptly overheated into a fiery blush when my brother demanded, "So, do you usually date your clients?"

I coughed, sputtering violently. My ever-helpful older brother patted me on the back, still watching Dylan and waiting for an answer.

Dylan's mouth quirked in the suggestion of a smile that didn't entirely materialize. "Is that really your concern?"

Eric grinned unrepentantly. "You'll find that, in the South, we have a broad view of what is our business. Especially when it comes to our kid sisters."

"Ah. Well, no, I don't make it a general practice to go out with clients. After watching my dad's friendship with his manager deteriorate, I decided professional and personal aspects of life were better kept separate."

Eric beamed. "Glad to hear it. Now, how about we go get real drinks? I love Mom and all, but why she'd mess up perfectly good bourbon with orange juice and other stuff…"

I hadn't quite recovered by the time they headed for the kitchen, apparently bonding. I planned to do my brother bodily violence next time he came within arm's reach of me…or thank him quietly. It wasn't a question I ever would have asked Dylan myself, but it was nice to know that I wasn't just standard operating procedure for him.

Of course, I wasn't sure where that left us, but my parents' party was not the place to find out. Seeing that I wasn't otherwise engaged in conversation, my mom towed several of her friends over to meet me.

I dutifully chatted with people for the rest of the evening, occasionally peering through the crowd to check on Dylan. He was most often found near one of my relatives, smiling at whatever they were saying. I tried not to speculate, figuring it would only lead to terror on my part.

Dylan gravitated back to my side as the party wound down. "Your family is a riot," he murmured near my ear.

"That's more diplomatic than what Amanda normally says," I whispered back. "I mean, she loves them, but…you know."

He nodded sagely, a few hours in their company more than enough to illustrate my point.

"I love them, too," I quickly added, not wanting to seem like a completely ungrateful daughter.

"And they're crazy about you. That makes them a good family in my book."

Agreed, although I did wish that none of them were looking to me to help with their marital problems. As we said good-night, Carrie pulled me aside to tell me not to worry about suggesting a recipe.

"I figured I'd try a whole bunch and see what works best," she confided as she shrugged into her jacket.

"Carrie, I'm not sure that's…"

Eric walked up to us, jingling his car keys. "Ready?" he asked his wife.

Dylan and I departed soon after, and he followed me back to my place in his car. There were all kinds of things we could have talked about—the signing, my family, his returning to Atlanta—but once we were alone in my dark apartment, all I really wanted to do was be in his arms again. I craved that even more than raspberry-ribbon pie, which I was known to crave on a semi-regular basis.

Still, I was a chef raised in the South. I couldn't keep the words "Did you want anything to drink or eat?" from escaping. It was a stupid question, considering all the refreshments my mom had foisted on us, but what can I say? The hospitality gene is in my DNA.

He shook his head, trailing me into the living room. "Actually, all I really want is to kiss you." His smile flashed white in the dim illumination provided by the one living-room lamp I'd left on. "Openmouthed, if that's not beyond gross."

I laughed, but the sound softened to a sigh as he lowered his head toward mine. "I think I could be persuaded."

DESPITE DYLAN'S teasing promises to fix breakfast on the mornings he woke up here, I made brunch Sunday while he showered. I'd showered with him yesterday but told him when we finally rolled out of bed today that a stack of pancakes was not going to make itself while we ran up my water bill. The truth was, I just wanted a few minutes alone. His leaving in the next couple of hours was hitting me harder than I'd expected.

You're being silly. You'll see him in a few days.

We'd ordered take-out last night—we'd been far too worn out to contemplate cooking—and had talked over dinner.

He'd sprawled across the foot of my bed, bowl in hand as he lifted mu-shu pork to his mouth with expert maneuvering of his chopsticks. Then again, I'd already known how adroit the man's fingers were. "Miriam, you remember when I told your brother I liked to keep the professional and personal separate?"

I had nodded, staring intently into my lo mein.

"For the record, I consider this strictly personal. My job here was mostly over when you did that first cable interview. There's really no other advice left for me to give you on your remaining appearances...like the one in Atlanta."

My eyes had met his. "I don't know how busy you are, but I—"

"Stay with me," he'd invited, his tone too firm for it to be a question. "The least I can do is put you up for the night after you've let me stay here, right? Although I should warn you, there's no guest bed and the sofa pull-out is extraordinarily uncomfortable, so you may have to bring yourself to share *my* bed."

After that, the take-out had grown cold as I proceeded to accept his offer and express my gratitude.

"Something smells wonderful," Dylan said from behind me, jolting me back to the present.

I pressed a palm to my heart. "You startled me. My mind wandered, and I didn't hear you."

He was running a towel over his damp hair, looking entirely too masculine and sexy for my small kitchen and quaint breakfast of pancakes and eggs. It was like Betty Crocker meets a men's cologne ad.

"I'm guessing you don't usually let your mind wander when you're cooking?" he teased as he walked around the counter that opened into the dining room and took a seat. "I imagine you'd get a lot of entrées sent back to the kitchen if you did."

I dished up our breakfasts, setting his plate in front of him. "That's not really a problem since I don't *have* a kitchen. Professionally, anyway. I need to look for a job." I also needed to finish the second manuscript Hargrave was waiting for, but one thing at a time.

Dylan sprinkled pepper across his eggs. "What about my suggestion? Being famous is a job."

I laughed. "So is being an astronaut, but let's stick with something that's relevant to me."

Conversation tapered off while we ate, and I was glad the food gave me an excuse not to talk. I was feeling blue. Even though I knew I'd see him soon, his leaving today felt like a reality check. Dylan, back to his world. Me...no longer sure which world was mine. I wasn't Trevor's unappreciated sidekick any longer, that was for damn sure. Neither did I believe I was destined for sexy stardom; I was the last person who craved the spotlight for long-term periods. I'd been happy back in the kitchen, busily creating out of sight and running my own little kingdom.

Dylan, thoughtful man that he was, helped me clean the kitchen after we ate, but when we finished, he pulled me into a hug with a sigh. "I should take my leave before I'm tempted to put it off any longer. I hadn't planned to stay this long."

"I know." I pressed a kiss to his collarbone, not trying to "tempt" him, but just because I loved the contact. All right, and possibly to tempt him a tiny bit.

He gave me a look of mock reprimand. "None of that, now. Wicked woman."

It sounded so endearing when he said it, and so true. As if I were someone different with him just because he saw me that way. I felt a little pang of sympathy for Carrie, realizing fully what she'd meant now. Her complaint wasn't that Eric didn't love her, or even that he wasn't—not that I needed to know—expressing some physical affection…just that he wasn't looking at her as someone desirable. Dylan made me feel extremely desirable, but at times—mostly when we were outside the bedroom—I also felt like a bit of a fraud.

Too soon, we were exchanging our goodbyes. I forced brightness into my smile when I gave him a cheerful wave and told him I'd see him later this week.

He kissed me one last time before climbing into his car. "Call me after your trip to North Carolina."

I laughed. "You may not officially be my media consultant anymore, but old habits die hard, huh? Want to hear how the public appearances go?"

"No. Just want to hear from you."

I floated back inside, feeling like a well-loved woman.

Full of purpose, I sat down at the small desk in the corner of my bedroom and booted up my computer. I hadn't had a lot of enthusiasm for writing this book, but the check I would get after turning it in would give me some temporary latitude as I hunted for a new job. Besides, what better time to write a sexy, sassy sequel than after the weekend I'd just had?

Three hours later, I hadn't typed a single new page, although I had read lots of archived articles at the Web sites of some of my favorite food magazines. Research, I assured myself. It was harder to justify the half hour of solitaire, mindlessly moving cards around with the mouse while replaying scenes of Dylan and me in my head, as if we'd suddenly become my favorite late-night movie. Abandoning the pretense of working, I pushed my rolling chair away from the computer and tossed myself onto the unmade bed. I lay there for a moment, breathing in Dylan's scent on the sheets.

Pathetic.

I sat up, thinking that maybe I'd give Amanda a call, but I surprised myself by dialing my brother's number instead.

"Hello?"

"Hey, Carrie. It's me." At her lengthy pause, I added, "Miriam."

"Oh. Duh, sorry about that. Did you want to talk to Eric? He's chasing the girls around in the backyard."

"That's okay, I called to talk to you."

Another pause. "Everything okay?"

"Yeah, I just thought we could chat."

"You're *sure* everything's okay?"

"It's fine." I laughed, guessing I must call Carrie even less than I'd realized. "Well, Dylan left today, which kind of sucks, but I'll see him later this week."

I could hear the smile in her voice when she spoke. "So you've finally been bitten again by the love bug? Thank God. Trevor didn't deserve you."

As much as I wanted Carrie to know me, I was hesitant to discuss my feelings for Dylan right now until I figured out just what was happening between us. "Hey, you know what I thought might be fun? I have one last local television spot tomorrow, but I'm free all evening. Think Eric could keep the kids and we could go see a movie?"

She laughed. "So your mom was right. Amanda finally *has* found a steady boyfriend."

"That has nothing to do with it," I protested. "In fact, I could even see if she wants to join us." Mondays were a slow day at the bar, and it was likely she had the night off. Of course, whether or not she and the dapper Richard already had plans…

"That would be wonderful," Carrie enthused. "I love my children, and I love my friends, but it would be kind of cool to spend the evening with a couple of women not in the PTA with me."

"Then it's a date!"

"Eric and the girls should be inside in a few minutes for dinner, so I'll let him know."

Dinner. I bit my lip. "You didn't, uh, make anything from my book, did you?"

She sighed, having apparently rethought her strategy since I'd seen her last Friday night. "No. I told the girls to pick what they wanted. Lyssa wanted fish sticks and Lana wanted Vienna sausages, so I cut them both up into some mac-n-cheese."

The chef in me gagged. "Well, that sounds…good."

Her giggle surprised me. "Are you kidding? It sounds awful. I'm having a salad. And Eric is free to eat whatever he'd like if a casserole planned by three-year-olds doesn't appeal to him. But he'll be fixing it for himself."

DYLAN'S UNLIKELY COMMENTS about imminent stardom aside, it was clear from our girls' night out that nobody would be basing any witty new sitcoms on Carrie, Amanda and me. We did not possess the worldly, humorous air often seen in television gal pals.

Carrie got up twice during the movie to call home and check on Lyssa, who'd been running a low-grade fever that day, and I was too annoyed by my own day to enjoy the comedy we'd chosen to see. I'd had one last South Carolina station that had agreed to have me on to promote my book, but the whole time I had been there, I'd wanted to ask the cameraman if I could borrow his light meter to shove it down the host's throat. Whereas Stephen had been flirtatious during our dialogue, and Ashlee had been like a gossipy friend eager to exchange secrets, this host, Clark Cooper, was a condescending putz.

Every question about my book had been a thinly disguised insult. For instance, had I written it for all those women out there who needed help catching a man? Wasn't I worried that the sexy tone was sending the wrong message to young women who looked to me as a role model?

Please! I wasn't exactly a household name, and my books were shelved in the cooking section, not children's literature. Nor did I think my book was racier than some of the provocative headlines on magazines stocked in every single grocery checkout line in the zip code. The entire experience had left me wanting to go find his car in the parking lot and let the air out of his tires. I had hoped that the evening out with Carrie and Amanda would boost my spirits; this plan might have been more effective if either one of them had been feeling better.

Amanda was a wreck. "I can't do this," she told us over post-movie milk shakes at a retro diner meant to evoke a fifties soda shop.

Things with Richard were going incredibly well. Since his daughter had been out of town for the weekend, he and Amanda had finally made love. She'd confessed to us that there was a definite upside to dating a slightly older man who had accumulated more years of experience and know-how than most of her past boyfriends. Unfortunately, things were going so well that he wanted to take her to his parents' home for dinner. Rather, his parents' mansion, as he came from an extremely wealthy family.

"They're going to hate me," Amanda wailed.

Sitting next to her in the booth, Carrie patted my friend's hand reassuringly, sending me a discreet, "do something!" glare. Fair enough. Amanda was my best friend, after all.

"I can't believe you're even worried about this. Everyone loves you," I told her. "You're a fabulous person and have no reason to feel insecure."

"Well, there was no one important enough to be insecure over."

Her response resonated inside me, as I thought about how nervous I was about seeing Dylan this week, about broaching the subject of our relationship.

But this was about Amanda. "Just be yourself," I told her. "And maybe bring a side dish to dinner with you to show how thoughtful you are. Then they'll know their son is with a caring woman. Between that and the fact that his daughter likes you, they should be reassured."

"A side dish? You'll make it for me, won't you?"

"Come over before your dinner, and we'll make it together," I suggested.

"Okay. And maybe I can borrow some of your clothes?"

"My clothes?" We weren't exactly the same size.

She ran a glance over the colorful, recently purchased sweater I was wearing with a comfy pair of old jeans. "Well, not your new clothes. The boring ones."

Carrie smothered a laugh, then offered her own take on the situation. "Did you play any of those stupid games with Richard? The kind where you act like you love football because he does, or you don't eat dessert in front of him so he won't think you're a pig?"

Amanda snorted, looking more her normal self. "Hardly."

"That's what I thought. You didn't pretend to be anything other than exactly who you are. He loves you as-is, and that's the person you should be when you meet his parents. If they care about him, all they want is for him to be happy. And if they don't care about their son's happiness, their opinion doesn't matter anyway, as far as I'm concerned."

I grinned at Carrie. "You're pretty smart, you know that?"

She nodded. "It's the perk of being an old married lady with kids. You acquire wisdom."

I blew my straw wrapper across the table in protest of her calling herself old, and the rest of the evening was mostly us being silly and giving each other a hard time. We concluded that we were definitely going to do this again, although Carrie said we couldn't have a girls' night until I'd written at least one new chapter because she didn't want to "contribute to the delinquency of an author."

As I was getting ready for bed that night, however, Carrie's earlier words came back to haunt me. *You didn't pretend to be anything other than exactly who you are.* Although I knew she'd meant them for Amanda, she'd made a good point about being yourself. If the person you were with had only been attracted to an image, how would they feel about the real you?

Wasn't that what I had been doing with Dylan? Pretending?

I'd never lied about who I was, but the entire time I'd known him, I'd been changing my appearance and behaving out of character. That transformation was the whole reason he'd come to South Carolina in the first place, and sometimes, with his talk about helping me live up to my potential or making me a star, I got the impression he was more enthusiastic about the new and improved me than I was. Our weekend together had been incredible, but would he have been so attracted to the "old me," the one I still was on the inside?

14

In the end, though, what you serve is usually a lot less important than who shares the meal with you.

THE ANNUAL NORTH CAROLINA food festival rocked—it was a weeklong event, although I couldn't afford to pay for a booth, so I only attended for my scheduled Tuesday evening activities. Nothing like being surrounded by a few thousand other people who loved food as much as I did to put a smile on my face. Most anyone can appreciate eating, but true food sensualists appreciate the textures, the aromas, the cultural significance, the preparing, the anticipation….

I got home very late Tuesday night and was awakened some time Wednesday morning by the ringing of the phone. My first joyful thought was *Dylan!* I'd promised to call him after the trip, and maybe he'd expected that to be last night. Maybe he was worried or wanted to hear the sound of my voice.

Then again, I thought, glancing at the digital clock on my nightstand, Dylan would know better than to call me at nine-thirty.

"Hello?" I mumbled into the phone, sounding as if I'd just been yanked out of a deep sleep.

"Miriam? This is Joan," my editor greeted me. "Did I wake you?"

"What? No. I've been awake for…I've been awake. I was just, um, working." Uh-oh. She must be calling to ask how the new book was coming. "It's almost done! That's right. I was working on the second book, and it's almost done."

"Great." She cheerfully accepted my heinous deception without so much as a pause, so perhaps I was a better liar than I thought. "The public will be clamoring to read it, especially after I give you my news. Rona wants you. Rather, *Six Course Seduction.* It's her Valentine's Pick."

Brain fog prevented me from celebrating this joyous announcement. Who the heck was Rona?

I didn't actually voice the question, but the silence must have betrayed my utter confusion.

"You do know who Rona Montgomery is, don't you?" Joan prompted. "She was discovered on some reality show a couple of years ago and has her own daytime program now."

The penny dropped—right, I'd heard of her. If she'd been a nighttime talk show host, I would have recognized her name instantly. But she'd apparently been on some televised challenge show and America had found her endearingly plucky, enough to give her an hour in the afternoons to talk about various subjects and meet with occasional members of the entertainment industry with a new project to plug.

"Right, Rona. Sure."

"Well, she's made it a point to say that even though television is her home, she thinks people should take more time to read. Every major holiday, she recommends a thematically related book. On Saint Patrick's Day, she 'discovered' a new novelist with Irish roots, at Christmas, she listed two young-adult novels that would make perfect gifts for kids, and for Valentine's Day—"

"She's recommending *Six Course Seduction.*"

"Right! Isn't this the best news? She has a nationally syndicated show. We might even be able to get you a guest appearance with her when your second book comes out!"

Yipes. That would require my writing a second book someday soon.

"Great! Hey, can I call you back, Joan? I left the oven on." Stupid—ovens can easily be turned off while you talk on the phone. "I mean, I have a pot boiling over. Big mess. I should really go...."

My editor was either very indulgent because of the good news, or she was simply used to dealing with harmlessly crazy authors, because she didn't question my half-coherent state or lame excuse to get off the phone.

Once I'd showered and dressed for the day, the fact that my defiantly written cookbook might actually become a nonfiction bestseller started to sink in. I decided I wanted to share the good news. Also, I was desperate to hear Dylan's voice.

"Dylan Kincaid speaking."

I smiled at the now-familiar non-accent that always made me a little more aware that I was from South Carolina. It wasn't that he sounded British, really, he just sounded like a guy you would never ever hear use the word *y'all.*

"Hi. It's Miriam."

"Impostor! Miriam didn't have any public appearances scheduled today that I know of—and I can think of no other reason she'd be awake before eleven."

I laughed. "You're awake, and you aren't exactly a morning person yourself."

"The evils of having clients—they largely determine your schedule. I'm on the way to meet one in Marietta now. Besides, it's considerably easier to get out of bed when there isn't a sexy woman enticing you to stay in it." His tone became less teasing. "I miss you, you know."

Excitement arrowed through me. *Tomorrow.* By tomorrow evening, I'd be in his arms.

Almost as if he could read my thoughts, he drawled, "You could always come up tonight, stay over at my place and show up for your interview rested, instead of driving in tomorrow morning."

I grinned. Rested? Who did he think he was kidding? "Trust me, it's tempting. But Amanda's coming over for a cooking lesson tonight, and it's important. Besides, I really, really need to work on my book."

It was then that I got around to giving him my good news about Rona and her commitment to literacy, et cetera, et cetera.

"This is fantastic!" Dylan said. "Didn't I tell you? The book is wonderful. *You* are wonderful. This could be a springboard for—"

"I'm going to get springboarded to the top of my editor's shit list if I don't write this second book they're paying me for."

"What have you got done so far?" he asked reasonably, no doubt prepared to help me break the daunting task into less intimidating goals.

"Um, so far? The dedication." Belatedly recalling that his friendship with my editor was how I'd met him in the first place, I quickly added, "But please don't mention that to Joan!"

"Mmm, blackmail potential. I like it."

"You are a bad man."

The rest of our conversation devolved mostly into suggestive taunts that made me light-headed when I remembered I'd be spending tomorrow night with him.

"I don't know how you expect me to concentrate during this meeting," he mock-complained. "But I'm glad you called. Have I told you recently that you are the sexiest woman I know?"

There was a traffic jam in my head of all the flippant jokes I could make to that statement, but they collided into one another and none of them made it out before he spoke again.

"You do know I'm mad about you?" he asked. Then he laughed softly. "I never would have predicted it the night we met, but I am."

A lump formed in my throat, but I managed to get out a goodbye past it. I didn't know if I was choked up over his admission or weepy because he wouldn't have thought it possible when he first met me...a woman who had stammered nervously and worn a bulky sweater that still hung somewhere in her closet. I was crazy about Dylan, too, but I was worried. He'd told me before that what people saw was what really mattered, even more than the truth sometimes. Would he have fallen for me without Bruce's haircut and Rona's endorsement?

I'd see him tomorrow. Maybe then I could assure myself that our relationship wasn't just style over substance.

"MIRIAM, COULD I SPEAK to you?"

A woman who wasn't the producer I'd met earlier, but who carried herself with obvious importance, addressed me as the technician was unfastening the mike box on the back of my shirt.

"Absolutely." I stood, smiling at the dark-haired woman in the blue blazer. "I'm sorry, did we meet earlier?"

"No, I was in a meeting before you went on the air

with Phyllis and Tom. Sarah Winters. I'm the station manager here." We shook hands, and Sarah ushered me toward a refreshment room that smelled like fresh coffee and stale doughnuts. "Can I get you anything to drink?"

When I politely refused, she asked if we could talk in her office. I had the impression of being asked to stay after class to see the principal. I followed, wondering if I'd done something wrong during the cooking segment or the interview portion where I'd been cutting up with the other guest, an Atlanta hockey player. Maybe I shouldn't have interrupted so much? His tough, manly persona had made him the perfect person to heckle about doing something romantic, like cooking for his girlfriend on Valentine's Day. He seemed to have enjoyed the banter, too, but perhaps Phyllis and Tom didn't appreciate being overshadowed on their own show.

Once we were seated on opposite sides of a sleek black desk, Sarah leaned forward, her chin steepled on her fingers. "Do you know who Luther Cox is?"

Never heard of him. "Should I?" I asked, my tone apologetic and my nose wrinkled.

"He owns a cable franchise, several stations across the southeast, including this one. You did a show for one of our affiliates last week—*Around the House with Ashlee?"*

I nodded, glad to have some idea of what she was talking about for the first time. "Sure. That was a blast."

"Good, good. And you enjoyed today's segment?"

I nodded again.

"Luther runs in some important New York entertainment circles and has recently become aware of your book. He was very impressed by the tape of your appearance on Ashlee's show and asked me to keep an eye on you today. The fact of the matter is, we're interested in offering you your own show."

"What?"

"You did a great job out there. You practically outshone your hosts, and I don't mean that as a criticism. Your joking around with the other guest, the flirtatious way you talk about your book—our viewers are going to eat that up. Luther seems to think that your cookbook is going to hit big, and we're offering a win-win situation. We capitalize on the name recognition once it sets in, and you get your own program. *Dishing: With Miriam Scott.* Combination cooking show and sex advice. Not explicit, of course. Just romantic tips with the occasional wicked comment. The same kind of thing you're already doing so well."

Except that people on live television should probably be quick on their feet, and I was dumbfounded.

"It would be here in Atlanta, and the money would be all right." She named a salary that wouldn't make me rich but would definitely be enough to live off. "Right now, it would be a local market, but if you ever hit nationally... You don't have to give me an answer now, Miriam, but think over the possibilities."

I took her card and may have said something by way of a farewell. It's equally possible that I staggered wordlessly out of her office and straight into the vending machine that sat in the hall.

My own show?

I would have to move.

Trevor would have an aneurysm when he found out.

I would probably have to get up before noon.

You'd be in the same city as Dylan. My heart leaped at the thought, but I didn't know if Dylan himself would have the same reaction.

He'd e-mailed me directions to his apartment, and despite my rather dazed state, I managed to find my way there. It was almost four o'clock by the time I pulled into the gated parking garage, using the visitor's code he'd sent me, and Dylan had told me to show up any time after two.

It was a nice complex, with its own pond and fountain on the grounds, slate-blue buildings and what looked like freshly painted white shutters. I had never bought into "image is everything," but improving his clients' images was obviously enough for Dylan to make a nifty salary. The buildings faced each other so that all the front doors opened into the breezeway where the stairs were located. The apartment I was looking for was on the second floor.

My heart hammered in my ears as I climbed. A month ago, I hadn't even known Dylan Kincaid, and now his face was etched in my memory, along with the sound of his voice, the taste of his kiss, and the fact that he stole the covers around four in the morning. Of course, last Saturday night, as I'd cuddled closer to reclaim a corner of the sheet, I thought I'd seen him grin.

I found the door with the gold numbers 206 on the front, and shifting the duffel bag on my shoulder, I knocked. Dylan's voice, deep but muffled, called out, "Just a minute," and then I heard quick, heavy footfalls.

The door swung open, and Dylan grinned at me, wickedly sexy in a black button-down shirt and black slacks. He was one eye-mask away from fulfilling a girl's Zorro fantasies.

Hm, foods for role-playing. *That* could be an interesting chapter.

I smiled at the source of my inspiration. "Hel—"

Cupping my face in his hands, he kissed me softly,

then with more hunger as we maneuvered our way through the doorway.

"—lo," I breathed.

His apartment had an honest-to-goodness foyer, and I smiled at the sight of the coatrack sitting on the tile, thinking of Dylan's first visit to my apartment.

He lifted the duffel bag for me, gallant as ever. "This is light."

"Well, I'm only staying the one night," I said sensibly.

"Don't remind me. Still, I've known a lot of women who would have needed a full-size suitcase just for hair products."

I wondered if these were women he'd known professionally or personally. "Yeah, well, I'm not that high-maintenance." Or hadn't been until recently. He didn't need to know about the time and energy I'd put into styling this morning. Unlike most men, however, instead of teasing, he probably would have applauded the extra effort. My image consultant would have been the first to remind me that you didn't just yank your hair back in a scrunchy for television.

The hallway opened into a living room with a kitchen on the right, another hall on the left, and a nice view onto what looked like a rolling, green golf course through the glass balcony doors. The living room itself was spacious, an expanse of gleaming hardwood beneath a skylight. A black leather couch that looked as if it had just been purchased today sat facing a television on a plain stand. I saw no evidence of an extensive tape or DVD collection, although there was a top-of-the-line stereo on the floor-to-ceiling bookcase. Wow, he hadn't been kidding about being an avid reader.

A little jolt of emotion tugged at my heart when I noticed *Six Course Seduction* had been added to the shelf.

"Can I get you anything?" he asked.

"Ice water would be great."

Utterly curious about his kitchen, I followed him to a room with enough faux-granite counter space to make me drool. He had an *island*. I suspected, however, that the pots hanging above it were largely ornamental, as the rest of the room was bare. Even Amanda had a toaster plugged in.

"You have no kitchen appliances," I said with a disbelieving laugh.

"I thought that's what the stove, fridge and dishwasher were," he said as he pulled down two clear blue glasses from a cherry-stained wooden cabinet.

"You have to at least own a coffeemaker," I chided.

"Oh, I do. Somewhere." He shrugged. "I'm not a big cook, and I travel a lot. When I am here, I have a lot of dinner and lunch dates. W-with clients."

I smirked.

His kitchen was big enough to accommodate an oval table and curvy wooden chairs with gold-flecked navy padding. We sat down with our water.

"So did you have any trouble finding the complex from the station? I wish I could've come and watched, but I was meeting with a businessman who is trying to soften his image before he offends half of his employees into working for the competition."

The station—that meeting in Sarah's office seemed like a weird dream. "No, I didn't have any trouble getting here. About the TV interview…"

Dylan frowned, looking worried. I'd e-mailed him a few curt remarks about the chauvinist who'd interviewed me on Monday. "Did it not go well? Are you—"

"It went great." A semi-hysterical giggle escaped. "So great they offered me a show."

He sat back in his chair, blinking. "I don't understand."

"They offered me my own cooking and romance show, *Dishing: With Miriam Scott*. The man who owns the station, Luther Cox—"

"*The* Luther Cox?"

I gave a feeble shrug, apparently alone in not having heard of the guy until today. "Unless there are more than one of them who own a bunch of television channels."

Dylan shot to his feet, grabbing my hands. "We have to celebrate! Anywhere in the city you want for dinner. What did Amanda say when you told her?"

I smiled at the way he automatically thought of my closest friend. "You're the first person I've told. I guess I'll mention it to everyone after I get back, but I have to think about it."

He looked stunned. "What is there to think about? This is exactly the kind of thing we were working toward."

I frowned. Since when? "I was just…my goal was to promote the book."

"Sure, but the book was a first step on this path. The timing couldn't be more perfect. You're quitting your job at the restaurant, right?"

"Well, yeah. But—"

"And this will be such fabulous exposure for the second book."

"Assuming I ever get it fin—"

"I told you, you had the potential! I knew it from the very beginning. You can be a star. You're funny and sexy, and your personality shines through whether it's on the page or—"

"Hold it." Things were going very fast, and my head was starting to spin. I tried to process a few fragmented thoughts. "What do you mean, 'from the very beginning'? You expect me to believe that you walked into that bar, where I was huddled with my book cover I didn't want anyone to see, tripping over my own tongue when I tried to talk, and you thought she's funny and sexy? Come on! You thought Amanda was the author."

He sat back down, his expression sheepish. "All right, so we had some changes to make. But the potential was always there. And you've transformed from—"

Logically, I knew he was trying to pay me a compliment, knew that Hargrave had *paid* him to come and transform me, but his words stung. "And now that I'm the sexy butterfly instead of the awkward caterpillar, you're attracted to me." Whereas I had been drawn to him from the beginning.

"That's not at all what I meant. It isn't as if you suddenly walked in with highlights in your hair one day and I fell for you. I told you, I felt a connection to you from the moment I read your book."

I sighed miserably. "But I BSed my way through that. I was mad at Trevor, and at least one sheet to the wind, and Amanda was egging me on, so I came up with an outline. Sheer reckless stubbornness helped get me through it. Half those things I suggested—I've never tried those. That book isn't me. At least, not all of me."

He looked insulted. "You don't think I realize there's a good bit more to you than a collection of recipes? Let's not argue. This is a night for celebrating."

I pursed my lips.

"You said yourself when I first got to South Carolina that sometimes you want to move far, far away from your family," he said coaxingly. "The show would be here in Atlanta?"

I nodded, noticing the eager emphasis he put on *here.* Clearly, I didn't need to worry that he wouldn't want me living in the same city. He seemed delighted by the prospect.

"But I don't even know if I want that."

His head drew back, his hands falling away from where they'd rested on my knees.

I hadn't meant that I didn't want to be closer to him. But he wasn't the only person in my life. "Charleston is my home. And I did say that about wanting to move away from my family. I'm not sure I meant it, though." Lately, I'd been realizing how much my friends and relatives meant. I'd even been trying to learn how to open up to them more—not *all* of the changes I was making were bad. But that didn't mean my dream career was getting up every morning, being layered in makeup and pretending to be some kind of sexpert while I prepared foods that weren't actually going to be served.

I'd been happy working as a chef. I missed the crew, the power of creation and knowing that what I was preparing had a direct effect on diners. Whether it was a spicy dish that made them feel daring for trying something new or a homey soup that reminded them of childhood or just a luxurious meal that was part of their celebrating some milestone. My food had been a part of all that.

"What if you gave it a trial run?" Dylan asked.

I shook my head, but he continued his argument.

"You worked hard on your book, we worked hard to promote it, and now you have the chance to—"

"There's a lot more anonymity in typing something outrageous at two in the morning than there would be standing in front of a camera crew and saying it."

"So you don't want to be successful because you're

suddenly shy?" He was incredulous. "Temporary camera fright is no reason to throw away a career opportunity we prepared for—"

If he'd sounded confused, I could have handled that. But what right did he have to sound angry? I stood. "I appreciate all you did to get me ready for a couple of interviews. But I'm not picking careers anymore based on the influence of the men in my life."

"That's highly unfair!"

"I suppose it was." Whatever problems I'd had with Trevor hadn't been Dylan's fault. Nonetheless… "I don't want to be worried about being 'sassy and sensual—'" punctuated with sardonic air quotes "—on a daily basis. Or deal with snotty attitudes about my media persona or with men who think my book gives them a right to leer. I just like to cook."

I felt deflated, wistful for what could have been and regretful that I'd gone so far down the wrong path. "These last couple of weeks have been fun, in their own stressful way. Exciting, like a vacation from my real life, you know? But I want to be Miriam again, wear whatever pants are comfortable at the time, even if they aren't the ones that best accentuate my hips, pull my hair back while I'm baking instead of worrying about what it looks like on camera. And I can't help feeling like that's not the girl you were involved with. Because if you *really* knew her, how much she values her privacy and how little she cares about appearances, you wouldn't have had the least bit of trouble understanding why becoming a television personality wasn't for me. So, as fun as this vacation has been, I think it's time I get back to reality."

"You're not staying the night?" His tone was feather-soft, but the anger was still there.

Tears clogged my voice. "I don't think that would be wise."

"I'll walk you out, then."

I almost smiled at this final act of familiar chivalry, but the expression cracked on my face, and I barely made it to my car before I started crying in earnest.

"MEN SUCK."

"You really think that's the best name for a restaurant?" Carrie glanced up from the legal pad on my dining-room table, the Saturday afternoon sun and her yellow cardigan making her look bright and cheery. Or maybe she had other reasons for the glow on her face today. I hadn't asked, because frankly, I didn't want to revel in anyone's happy romance right now.

"No," I answered. "Although we'd probably draw in a fair number of disgruntled women."

She laughed. "True, but why limit your clientele?"

My mood didn't lend itself to brainstorming today, but it had been my idea for Carrie to come over. I was sick of my own company and actually looking *forward* to going back to Spicy Seas on Monday…temporarily, at least. I'd heard through the grapevine that Trevor and Blondie had split up, leaving him with no prospects for a chef. I could bring in a salary while he interviewed for a replacement, giving me time to put my own plans into motion.

Because I'd barely slept since driving back to Charleston Thursday—and I definitely hadn't accomplished any writing—it had given me time to think about what I really wanted to do. I didn't want to work for Trevor, and I didn't aspire to eventually starring on the Food Network. I wanted my own place—a niche restaurant, something small and elegant with a specific, unique menu. Amanda, who had been ecstatic about the idea, had suggested an all-aphrodisiac menu and a restaurant name of The Love Shack. But Amanda wasn't here today, so I decided to overrule her vote in her absence. She had a girls' day planned with Richard's daughter. I understood she was taking Elizabeth to meet Bruce.

Carrie sighed. "Did you really want to work on this today, or did you invite me over so that we could talk, mind-blowing as that concept is?"

I grinned. "Since when are you so sarcastic?"

"Could be your influence." She returned my smile. "Eric says he's a little worried that we're suddenly becoming such buddies."

Guilt stabbed me. "You know I've always liked you, right? I mean, maybe we weren't exactly close before—"

"It's fine. I was a little too outspoken and perpetually cheerful for you. And it's not like I don't have plenty of friends. But it is nice that you're so much more...approachable, lately."

"As long as you hold to your promise not to describe anything my brother does in the bedroom, ever," I reminded her with mock fierceness.

My attempt at joking didn't fool her.

"You miss him," Carrie said quietly. We both knew who she meant. "You look as miserable as I've been feeling."

I arched an eyebrow. "I can't help but notice you look pretty chipper today."

She grinned.

"So you and Eric worked things out?"

"When I got home from dropping the girls off at a birthday party the other night, *he'd* made *me* brownies. Apparently, it's part of his new campaign to seduce his wife."

I laughed. "Glad to hear it, but what happened to cause the turnaround?"

"Miriam. Some things between a man and woman are private," she said archly. "So if you don't mind, I'm keeping the details to myself."

"Ha, ha. Have your fun."

She shrugged. "We talked, about a lot of things we've both been feeling. He admitted that *he's* been feeling different, older. He thought that by having another baby, maybe we could go back a couple of years. The girls are growing so fast…I convinced him that wild monkey sex was a much better way to stay young."

I cupped my hands over my ears. "I can't hear you!"

"Then that will make the taboo subject of Dylan a lot easier to broach," she said.

My hands fell to my sides. "Not much to say."

"There you go again. Sometimes, it is good for people to talk things out, even the annoying touchy-feely stuff."

I gave her a dry look. "I did tell him my feelings. That would be why I'm here, and he's in Atlanta. I think I made it pretty clear that I wasn't the person he wanted. And that his vision for me wasn't what *I* wanted."

"Well, good for you. But after you explained all that, did you talk about what you did want? Give him a chance to explain all the stuff he loves about you?"

"I—what was your point again?"

"I just hate to see you miserable. You weren't this upset when you broke up with Trevor."

"That's because Trevor was a clod, and I never should have confused his pursuing me for professional reasons as romantic pursuit."

"Maybe Dylan was the same way," Carrie theorized with a scowl. "Your media success was by extension his."

"No. I don't think he wanted me to be on television because it made him look good. He's a good guy, really kind and supportive. It's actually kind of sweet that he thought I had the potential to do this and wants to see me succeed. But just so you don't think your feeble attempt at reverse psychology was a total success, I still think it's creepy that my lover would encourage me to adopt a public persona of flirting with other men and making it sound like my sex life was an open forum."

"Damn. Still need to work on my subtlety, huh?"

I laughed. "Well, it wasn't a bad first effort."

AT TWO IN THE MORNING, when most normal people are sleeping, I was curled up on my sofa, watching one of the old *Planet of the Apes* movies. Okay, not really watching. More like, it was playing in the background while I sat and stewed over what Carrie had said earlier. It had taken me a while to really decide what I wanted to do with my professional life, and my own restaurant was it. It might be fun to continue doing some books, too, to promote the restaurant—although more books would definitely require getting my butt back in front of the computer sometime soon.

The thought of people trying my recipes in homes across the country was as exciting to me as a chef as being a part of people's lives when they came into my restaurant.

The question, though, was what did I want in my personal life? Rather, *who* did I want. The answer was immediate and heartfelt: Dylan Kincaid. That had really never been in doubt. The only thing I'd ever doubted was that he would want me. After all, he'd grown up around some exotic, glamorous people and loved to move from place to place and relationship to relationship. I, on the other hand, hadn't even been exciting enough to hold Trevor's interest.

And I didn't plan to reinvent myself to try to hold a man. Doing something new with my hair was one thing, but there was a limit to what I would do to make my image compatible with someone. Mostly because I didn't want to be with anyone who thought image was the important part.

On the other hand, while I may have felt like a fraud writing the first draft of *Six Course Seduction,* I hadn't felt phony with Dylan. The flirting between us hadn't been me practicing on him, it had just been his effect on me, the chemistry between us. And maybe anyone who writes a book feels those moments of "Who am I fooling? No one's going to want to read this," regardless of the subject matter.

Was that niggling insecurity really a good enough reason to have left Atlanta so quickly before giving Dylan a chance to talk everything over with me?

Carrie and my mom were both happily settled into relationships, and Amanda seemed to have found her own. According to the statistics I'd heard depressed single women mutter, there might not be all that many great guys still left out there. Was I an idiot for letting this one go, just because he'd wanted to see me do well?

I bit my thumbnail, glancing at the tiled end table where the phone rested. Could I call him? I knew he was a night person like me, but calling someone at two in the morning seemed—

Though the knock at the front door was soft, I jumped about a foot, my heart pounding wildly. Suspecting it was Amanda but wishing I had a baseball bat just in case, I glanced through the peephole in the door. The man standing on the other side did nothing to settle my heart.

I released the dead bolt and started to swing the door open, completely forgetting to unlatch the safety chain first.

Dylan smiled. "Does that mean I can't come in?"

My shaking hands fumbled with the chain. "You just...well, you caught me by surprise. It's two in the morning!"

"I knew you'd be up," he said affectionately as I finally got the door open. "So, *can* I come in?"

"Of course." To my knowledge, I'd never hallucinated before, but I was seriously wondering if I'd started now. Or if I'd fallen asleep on the couch.

He glanced to the television set, where *Apes* had given way to some infomercial for exercise equipment, back to me, taking in my rumpled hair and baggy navy sweats. "Exactly as I pictured you," he said in a self-satisfied tone.

"Um. Okay." Didn't sound like the fantasy that would prompt a man to drive through the night. "You just happen to be in the neighborhood?"

"No." He sat on my couch, and I realized for the first time how tired he looked, his eyes bleary and his jaw shadowed by stubble. "But I've barely slept the last couple of nights so I figured, hey, why not go for a drive? Coming here made as much sense as anything else. I miss you, and I hate the way we left things the other night."

I winced, knowing I was responsible for the terms of our strained goodbye. "I was going to call you about that, to apologize. I was nervous about seeing you, thrown by the station's offer...I reacted badly. So, I'm glad you're here."

"Glad because it gave you the chance to say you're sorry, or for other reasons?" His eyes were vivid and intense as they met mine.

"I—" For a moment, all I could think about was throwing myself into his arms. This was one sexy man who had crossed a state line to see me. "You've obviously been on the road for a few hours. Can I get you anything?"

He shook his head. "Just sit with me? I had a lot of time in the car to think about what I needed to say."

Since my body felt shaky, sitting was probably a good suggestion anyway. I swallowed. "I'm listening."

"Good. You know that motto they call the golden rule?"

"Do unto others?" I wasn't sure where he was going with this, but I figured I owed him the chance to speak his mind. Heaven knows *I* certainly had last time I'd seen him.

"As you would have done, yeah. But I think that suggestion is misleading." He ran a hand over his face, rubbing it along his jaw. "I hate to sound like the spoiled rich kid with famous parents or anything, because the fact of the matter is, I had a pretty good life. But they both made it clear that the spotlight was very important to them, and I used to wish they'd offer me just a little bit of that. Not so much because I wanted it, but because if someone had shared the attention with me, it would have meant *I* was important. I wanted that for you, Miriam—wanted you to have that chance to shine. I think you're terrific, and I guess I wanted you to have the opportunity to show the rest of the world that. Even if it was never what *you* wanted."

My heart melted. "Oh, Dylan. That's…nobody's ever said anything like that to me before."

"Well, I'm glad I followed up on my crazy idea of showing up in the middle of the night, then." He smiled fondly. "I did know you would be awake—comfy, probably watching something excruciatingly bad on television and managing not to get any writing done on your book."

"Hey!" I laughed at the accurate assessment.

"I do know you," he said. "But I'd like to get to know you even better. Be warned, though, that would probably lead to my falling more in love with you."

Tears stung my eyes, even though my smile grew even wider. "I love you, too. How could I not, with the way you treat me, the way you look at me?" I shivered as he traced his fingers over my hand. "The way you touch me…"

He seemed considerably more alert and energetic than he had when he'd first stepped inside the apartment. "I told you that I move around a lot."

The reminder poked a little hole in my bubble of happiness. It would be hard to run my own restaurant if I were traveling the globe, and hard to sustain a relationship with a lover who was never around. "Yeah, you mentioned that."

"Well, I lied about it a little. I told you I enjoyed it, and I do at times, but there are moments when it feels lonely. As if the reason I'm really moving from place to place is because no place is really home. Maybe I could give Charleston a try. I hear the people are very welcoming."

Joy lit up inside me, and I suspected I was glowing the same way Carrie had been when she'd been over earlier. "Seriously? Because I know this chef who's decided she wants to open her own restaurant. She might have a question or two about designing an image and promoting it."

He smiled as soon as I mentioned the restaurant, but quickly made his expression stern. "I don't know if I'll be able to assist her. See, I have this philosophy about mixing personal and professional relationships."

I leaned toward him, letting my body brush his as

much as possible. "Isn't there anything I could do to change your mind?"

His grin was wicked. "Now that you mention it, I'm curious to try a couple of things I read about in this delightfully naughty cookbook."

Suddenly filled with long-absent inspiration—not to mention so much emotion I could pop—I shot him a grin of my own. "You think *that* cookbook was full of good suggestions, just wait until you read the sequel."